Momaya Annual Review
2006

A Momaya Press Publication

London, U.K. & Gaylordsville, Connecticut, U.S.A

First published in the United States of America, 2006 by Momaya Press. The moral right of Momaya Press has been asserted.

Printed and bound in the United States.

ISBN 978-0-6151-3469-7

Table of Contents

* Honorable Mention

List of Illustrations

Foreword

Welcome to the 2006 Momaya Annual Review. The work published in this volume you will not find published elsewhere. Our aim is to find writers that you have not read before – and hopefully provide the launch platform for these writers to become the authors whom you will read again and again.

There are two principal parts to our publication. First, stories around the theme of "Escape." Second, the winning stories from our 2006 Momaya Short Story Competition.

Every year we choose a theme to inspire writers and give coherence to the Momaya Annual Review. This year, the theme was "Escape." This theme is common to us all. Sometimes we long to escape a boring job, a loveless marriage, and distressed family situation. Sometimes we need to escape a prison, a repressive regime, a burning building. Escape can be dramatic, funny, dangerous, exciting, traumatic. Think of "Kavalier and Clay" by Michael Chabon, "Empire of the Sun" by J. G. Ballard, "Vernon God Little" - by D.B.C. Pierre, "The Handmaiden's Tale" by Margaret Atwood. The authors published here have tackled the theme from many angles: matricide, political asylum, and humour.

Momaya Press supports the short story as an art form by sponsoring an annual short story competition for new authors. This 3rd annual Momaya Short Story Competition built on the success of past years with a greater number of varied submissions. Congratulations to our winners, who were chosen from a pool of 189 submissions (an increase of 7% on the number of submissions we received in 2005, despite a shorter entry period). Authors submitted stories from eighteen countries around the world (an increase of two countries from 2005): Australia, Belgium, Bosnia and Herzegovina, Canada, China, France, Ireland, Israel, Italy, Lebanon, New Zealand, Nigeria, Singapore, South Africa, Spain, Switzerland, United Kingdom, and the United States. Women accounted for 60% of the entries, and many writers chose to submit multiple stories.

We founded Momaya Press in order to encourage people to both write and read short stories. We believe that the challenging, funny, and entertaining stories in this volume will inspire you to evangelize short stories. We hope you will share these stories with other readers, and we encourage you to write short stories yourself.

Our thanks to our judges, whose support enables a credible vetting of submitted stories: Claire Nozieres, a literary agent at Andrew Nurnberg Associates; Rosalind Porter, an assistant editor at Random House; and Lucy Alexander, a writer at The Times. The judges were impressed with the high overall quality of the entries, which made it difficult to single out the winners.

We hope you enjoy reading these stories, and that you will submit your own stories in future Momaya Short Story Competitions.

Maya Cointreau and Monisha Saldanha
Directors
Momaya Press
www.momayapress.com

The Glimmering

(Honorable Mention)

By Brad Adams

I am behind her and she is on her knees. There is a tattoo on her back of a tree, a trunk beginning at her butt and sprawling up her spine, branching at her shoulders. Her entire genealogy is laid before me; on the withered leaves there are names of her ancestors back to the 17th century when the Dutch colonists built a dam to protect their city. I am trying to figure out why she is wearing a belt. I can't do this but I am. This is hard but I'm not. Her peach underwear glow in the black-lit room. She is wearing a wig, her breasts are obscenely large. She is a caricature of male fantasy. She tells me that her bra size is a G.

For research; we decided to eat mushrooms and walk around the neon city. The canal water snaked around forever and we held hands and my wife told me that the mushrooms tasted like sticks. She grimaced as she gnawed on a dried mushroom button. She was waiting for the effects to take hold. There were a hundred different languages here, some unspoken, and people dissolved into one another with little contact. Bright red windows were opened and closed. Curtains were drawn; the pine-bitter smell of pot was ubiquitous in the air.

There is a pile of paper towels overflowing from the trash, an assortment of condoms spread out next to the bed. There is electronic music pulsating through the walls. We talk about something and her teeth are glowing under the black light, some brighter than others. I avoid looking at us in the mirror and we ask her some questions that she answers with three word answers. Her English is not so good.

For research, we decided to eat more mushrooms the next day and ride on a boat into the harbor. The days were gray and brown, the boat was crowded with different languages, most of them spoken, some of which I could not guess the origin. We held hands and I liked to think that I could guess where people are from just by hearing them speak. I pulled a flask from my jacket pocket and chugged warm tequila. There were people from France, Germany, England, Ireland, Italy, Canada, Belgium, Holland, and America on the boat that was floating in the harbor amidst house-boats and ships carrying cargo from across the world.

I want to the see the sperms; she says working the inside of my thighs, the other hand grabbing at my dick. How does it make you feel, she asks, and there aren't words for me to say. You show me the sperms, she says, to make the twins. She knows I can do it, and she is perched on her knees, her cartoon breasts not moving and there is a stark contrast between my pale skin and her brown body. I can see the heavy scars on the under side of her breasts, a darker brown, raised skin. The breasts are solid, but void of milk.

The art museum was full that day because it was raining a dull, cold rain. There was a large model house inside the museum, its walls detailed with tiny portraits, its floors covered with elaborate mini-rugs. We see each other floating above the ground in the reflection of the glass but the museums other patrons don't notice. I told my wife a funny joke and asked her marked, interesting questions without answers. We took pictures of the Rembrandt painting even though it was forbidden. Later, we had the picture of the picture developed and hung it on the walls of our white-walled apartment.

She is pinching me now, which causes me to go soft. Even the rubber can't dull the pain of her fingernails digging into the flesh above my stomach. She is reaching for my nipples. She can't know that I hate this; that I hate having my nipples pulled at like I am an animal that needs milking. These aren't the words that need to be spoken.

My wife gives me more mushrooms and we walk the streets. There are hallucinations of past Presidents swimming in the water, each in sync with the other, swimming to the lyrical sounds of lettuce being chopped. She asked me what the inherent differences between pornography and prostitution are and I wasn't able to answer. The two seem intertwined. Prostitution exists in every relationship. The transaction may not be palpable; the outcome may not be the same. But we trade our ability to fuck for a sense of power, security, and passion. Then we have pornography to remember the base activities and broadcast it for others to see.

She pulls down the front of her glowing peach panties and there are more tattoos on her pubic bone. It is her family crest, two lions grappling for a shield covered in flames. This tattoo is one color; green from when the ink met the skin. She is still wearing a baseball cap that helps to secure her platinum blond wig. Her hair is black underneath. She is showing me inside with the other hand pinching the inside of my thigh.

We drank tequilas and sucked on limes. Our hands were still salty when we left the bar. She asked me why I thought we all spoke different languages and commented how odd unfamiliar human language sounds without the ability to decipher its meaning. A passing person spoke and it sounded like they were clearing their throat. Snarf, snarf, snarf, snarf. A man was manhandling a baby in the streets. There were bright orange signs all around. I asked her if by sleeping with another woman, would it ruin us. I grabbed her ring finger and twisted her ring several times, rubbing my thumb over the diamond.

She is on her knees again and I am behind her. She tells me she used to be a full B cup and she wanted to go bigger than a G but it was not possible. Her breasts might explode all over me, I think, trying to finish. I want to escape. There is no feeling. She wants to see my sperms and tells me she is better than the Viagra, speaking to me from a script she wrote a year ago, that is shoved down into her knee high boots with my money. I still don't know why I am doing this. Were not going to make our train. I look below her to see my wife, naked and beautiful, her hands reaching up for mine. She has Renaissance paintings replicated on each of her nails, from Boticelli to Van Eyck. The detail is remarkable, the pious Mary sulking at Jesus worn feet. I study the soft muted colors of the Birth of Venus on her ring fingernail, Venus coyly covering her womanhood, her exposed pale breasts the focus of her plump body. My wife reaches up and touches the woman's large breasts; I reach around too and grab my wife's hands. There is a moment of passion, an electric shock of lust that makes my pelvis quiver. I turn over my shoulder and look at my back in the mirror. There us a roadmap of Queens tattooed on my back complete with updated MTA metro stops in red and green. In the black-lit room, I can envision where Brooklyn would be, its northern most neighborhood disappearing into my scalp. My wife's nipples are visible to me now as woman's back is turned and she is squatting at the head of the bed. I want you to fuck her, she tells me, and grabs my wife's breast with both of her hands.

We were late for our train. The planes stopped leaving late that night. There was an electric ocean glimmering below the two hundred ton metal planes. There were movies playing on the planes, there is fantasy and there is reality outside of the windows. We are spent. We have spent. There is nothing we can do to go backwards. But we ran towards the trains platforms, showing our tickets to a man who snarfed and let us pass. The interior of the train was green, a psychedelic lime green, and it rumbled under us and lurched forward. The mushrooms had worn off and I grabbed my wife hands. I did not pretend that night that I could understand what she was saying.

The Hangers

By Shannon Banks

You know those annoying women who seem to have the perfect lives? They are the ones who are both super wives and successful career women within one perfect package. They have a beautiful house, two perfect children (one boy and one girl), handsome and supportive husbands and dress in a designer but understated wardrobe. They have manicured nails on both their fingers and toes. They keep in touch with their friends, and are members of the local women's group.

Not only that, the perfect woman has time to do yoga. She is a 5'9" brunette with a fabulous figure. She has an exciting and successful career as a lawyer in the City. And on top of this, she keeps the perfect home. She loves to cook (and when she does, it's both gorgeous and tastes amazing), has a landscaped garden, and her house is picture perfect. No de-clutter therapy is needed for the perfect woman-every surface is pristine, every cupboard organized. The floors are polished, the shelves are dusted and the paperwork is in order.

This is a true confession. I used to be one of those women. Well, at least I thought I was. Or thought I should be. Anyway, there were no cracks in the veneer and everyone thought I lived the perfect life.

But then everything changed because of a wire hanger.

With my high-class lifestyle of perfection and the wardrobe that went along with it, I did a lot of dry cleaning. I mean, do you expect that I would hand-wash my Prada blouses? I loved to come home with a freshly cleaned wardrobe, my favourite black trousers hanging up and covered in a plastic bag, along side a selection of pressed blouses and jumpers. But every time I came in with my fresh, clean clothes, I brought back a new addition to my unwanted hangar collection.

I had an almost perfect process for putting away my dry cleaning. I transferred each shirt or pair of perfect size eight trousers onto a wooden cedar hangar and placed it in the appropriate section of my closet. My closet was organized by clothing type--shirts and blouses on the half-height rail on the left, trousers, dresses and skirts on the right--and then by colour. My friend Carrie organized by designer as well, but I always thought that was a little over the top.

Anyway, once my clothing was transferred to the rail, I was left with the standard cleaner-provided aluminium hangar, with its sharp wire end that attacked my hand when I carried the clothes upstairs to my dressing room. Sometimes the wire would be partially covered by a cardboard clothes protector or there would be some safety pins attached, but other than those minor variations, each was the same; each created disorder in my otherwise perfect life.

Originally, I tried to throw the hangars away. I bent them into two so they would fit into the small plastic waste bin in my dressing room, but the stiff wire insisted on returning to its original form, and would spring out on to the floor, with a life of its own. I didn't like this approach anyway, because the perfect woman is environmentally conscious, and I didn't feel right about just tossing them. So, one Monday when I came back from the cleaner and shifted my D&G jumper onto a cedar hangar, I hid the wire counterpart on the pristine (obviously) upper shelf in my closet, just out of my line of sight. "I can always take that down and recycle that later," I thought to myself. "Or maybe I'll even need it for when a guest comes to stay."

It started out as an innocent temporary step. Really. I had every intention of finding a new home for this annoying piece of wire. But since I couldn't exactly throw it away, what else could I do?

Then the breakdown started. On Thursday, I brought home some grey trousers, and found myself with the same dilemma. Not sure what else to do, I averted my eyes, and balanced the newest addition on top of its cousin in crime.

The following week, it was the same story-I looked the other way, and added to the pile.

Weeks passed, and two hangars became five, then ten. I did some research on the internet and found some charity organizations that might take them. "I should give them a call," I thought, but I was on my way out and was running late, so I couldn't do it just then. One afternoon, I bought home my cleaning, and as I went through my regular hangar-trading ritual, I found a black skirt mixed in with my white blouses. Shocked by this lack of attention on my part, I started to move it to its proper location, but then I noticed the green shirts were mixing with the blue ones too, so left the rogue skirt where it was, vowing to straighten the whole thing up on the weekend.

The weekend came and went and the hangar pile continued to grow along with the other chaos in my wardrobe. I started adding an occasional black plastic skirt hangar to the jumble of aluminium, and the odd plastic dry cleaner bag. It got so bad that I had to stand on tip-toe to reach the top of the wire pile, which was turning into a modern design sculpture in my closet.

The pyramid of twisted wire balanced precariously on the upper shelf for months, growing gradually more and more unsteady, until finally, when I shifted a black dress onto a cedar hangar and added the newest wire addition to the pile, it tumbled from the top, pulling down dozens of others from the collection with it like the childhood game Barrel of Monkeys. I protected my head as the hangars clattered around me onto the floor, pulling down the plastic skirt hangars and the dry cleaning bags--and a few handbags I had stashed up there the week before, as well as some t-shirts that I meant to give to my sister and some books I was going to give to a local charity shop.

When the avalanche finally stopped and I looked around at the chaos I had created, I realized that it wasn't just my wardrobe that was no longer immaculate. But more importantly, I discovered that I didn't care. So I stood there, in my dressing room, surrounded by my once-categorized designer wear and the tangle of wire at my feet, and I started to laugh.

That was it, the official end of my life of perfection. Once the hangars started falling, I found I didn't want to stop them. I made new friends who shopped in the sale racks at the Gap. I let my nails chip. I ate chicken chow mien from the Chinese around the corner, and I gained five pounds. I slept in and missed my 6am yoga class, and skipped a women's networking meeting to spend time in the park. I was passed over for the big promotion because I said I wouldn't work every weekend in May. But I found that I cherished the paperwork piles that accumulated on the kitchen counter. I put postcards on the fridge, even if it meant obscuring the clean lines, and I put out a vase to display the dandelions the kids picked from the garden.

Over time, the cracks in the veneer became wider and wider, and the real me stepped out.

Nasma's Malady

(Honorable Mention)

By Jo Cannon

From time to time something happens to me. Strange seizures come like migraines. First there is a sense of thinning, a delicate disruption, where my skin touches air. Boundaries blur until I no longer know where I end and other people begin. Often this feeling vanishes after a few seconds; sometimes it lasts all day. My mind is capsized by the thoughts of others. Crowded places confuse me because truly I cannot hear myself think.

I was not always like this; these bouts, like the menopause, began because it was my time. At first I mistook the hot slide on my skin as illness. But I knew something else had happened when the radio by the bed began to broadcast news I could feel. A flaw from outside had entered me. Listening to reports of a plane crash, I felt myself fall from the sky. Suicide bombs came nearer until they exploded inside my chest. The anguish of dying mothers and lost children overwhelmed me. During these times I cannot distance myself from suffering. Like a landslide, it buries me.

Outside I feel better -- I can breathe. At this time of year night falls early but I am never frightened. A middle-aged woman in a shabby coat attracts no attention in a city. And nothing can happen to me that has not already happened; nothing can be taken that I have not already lost.

I know the shape of each hour as night passes on these streets. In January by five o'clock children have returned from school and most people are bolted inside their houses. Shutters blind the shop windows. The doctor's surgery remains open but patients in the waiting room are uneasy; they want to be home, away from the darkness. They shuffle their problems -- headaches that come and go, breathing difficulties -- so the doctor will understand. When I pass the surgery other people's symptoms jangle in my head.

By seven o'clock there is a different feeling on the street, a change in the air. Shadows thicken beyond pools of streetlight. Boys too old for play stations or after-school lessons at the mosque clutter the door of the off-license. Around them slide sharper, denser shapes of older boys: teenage gangs. Voices suspended in mist erupt suddenly into laughter or glassy fury. I slip past quickly and they barely notice me. There is a hum, a tension, across my shoulders and down my arms while our minds fuse. For a second I feel their hostility and longing. Then I pull free and only the wind blows through me.

At eight the doctor leaves the surgery, rolling a shutter down over the door. All day his liturgy of duties warded off sadness. Now, as I pass unseen, his troubled thoughts open inside me like flowers. He thinks his wife no longer loves him; perhaps she will leave. Her eyes meet his with a new, calm withholding of expression. He knows the man, can picture them together. And suddenly it is too much: his wife, the procession of anguished stories he hears - how can he contain it? Every day he talks to people washed up from anywhere. Questions he cannot ask hang like bubbles in air. Why are you here? What has happened to you?

All he can say is, "Where does it hurt? Can you sleep at night?"

Sometimes I go to see him. When I told him about my malady he listened. He is a good man, he tries, but has heard nothing like it.

He said, "Nasma, women of your age. Your life has been difficult, sometimes the mind plays tricks. And you don't sleep enough. I'm worried about you."

Some nights I do sleep, but fever wakes me. I crawl onto Amos, lie on him like a raft. His arms come around me reflexively; his penis stirs slightly while he sleeps. I want to melt into the surface of his skin. But the attack is too strong: there is a sadness not my own, whispering voices. I have to get out of the house.

Our terraced house opens onto the street. Outside the front door is a gutted car. I have lived here eight years but know my neighbours only by sight. Many of the original elderly inhabitants have died. I recognise a pattern: an old person stops going out, the district nurse visits for a few months, then the doctor. Suddenly they are gone, the house occupied by someone else. A hurricane sweeps up people from all over the world and drops them on Popple Street. It is as good as anywhere. Scattered like salt, we do not understand each other. Our half-greetings are wary.

Nobody asks, "Why are you here? What has happened to you?"

Everyone waits for something to happen -- for life to regain meaning, or for hope enough to invent it.

This condition of mine is recent, no more than a year old. I have yet to discover whether it is infirmity or power. When I arrived in this country I was ordinary, powerless. Less than ordinary: nothing. At the immigration desk I rolled up my sleeves, pushed the shirt from my shoulders, showed my hands. Not my flesh -- surely somebody else's? The uniformed woman was shocked; her eyes flicked up to mine. I was taken away, examined by a doctor, then a lawyer. I am grateful. I was taken in, given shelter. This does not happen for everyone, but it did for me and I do not forget.

For years I couldn't believe my luck. I was safe, those men with mouths twisted like wire couldn't reach me. I believed I'd got away. And if I waited long enough Hasim would get away too: the hurricane would fling him down in Popple St. How could that not be true when he was with me all the time, even in dreams? In my thoughts I talked to him constantly, referring everything to him. If I flirted a little with someone, I imagined him jealous. I went to college, worked hard to learn English. Looking back I cannot believe I was like that -- I was a little mad. Sometimes I would glimpse the prison: a dark corner; a tail of anger that disappeared into somebody's eye; shouts on the street. And in nightmares, so I taught myself not to sleep. My body and face changed, became softer, middle-aged. I didn't mind, it was safer that way. Hasim would recognise me.

For a while my old life -- as teacher, rich woman, and Hasim's wife -- felt like a dream. My memories, of conversations mostly, were surreal. I used to be garrulous; friends and colleagues laughed at me because I never shut up. Hasim and I talked all the time. Here, closed up on myself like a folding chair, I rarely speak. When my English was good enough I got a job on a supermarket till. Nobody asked where I came from or why I was here; I couldn't believe that people with access to so much information could be so ignorant. And I met Amos, stacking boxes in the storeroom. My spurious confidence was beginning to slip: the memories I eluded had caught up and would soon overtake me. I began to see things, delicate as hair on a lens, in shadows and at night. Then all at once it was upon me. Heart racing, sweating, flooded by fear, I remembered everything that had happened. How had I failed to remember? In scarlet explosions, again and again, those men came back to claim me.

And like concrete filling a mould, came the slow, cold certainty that Hasim was dead.

I clung to Amos then. From the Congo, huge and slow moving, he asks nothing of me. His back is deeply gouged by knife or machete. Why are you here? What has happened to you? I have never asked. Sometimes his fingers trace my scars but he says nothing. His English is poor; we have no words to bind us. He walks as though on ground that might break underneath him, one careful step at a time. His massive male aura surrounds me, fills doorways, blocks light from windows like a sand bag. Amos would stop them. He would protect me.

Hasim's wrists were as thin as mine. He wept as they pushed us into different cars.

Amos whimpers in his sleep but I never wake him; I don't want nightmares to leach into his day. When headlights sweep the windows or there is sudden noise outside, sweat pours from him and I smell Africa on his skin. I watch over him, this stranger, uncertain which of us is stronger. When I come home from my night walks he is awake, waiting, fearful as a child. I let his body engulf mine. We have no words to comfort each other.

My life now is a book bent back along its spine. Two broken halves. Every moment two moments: before and after my arrest. I am not a brave woman; I gave them everything, did what they said, told all I knew. When they had taken all I had, they drove me to the airport and put me on a plane. But I brought the prison with me. Many times an hour I am back there. Triggered by a colour, a smell, a movement: cascades of connecting images that I have trained myself to step round. The present is lost -- a pause, a missed heartbeat -- as I keep the days going. And always I am vigilant. I do not allow myself to sleep for long.

Midnight. As I open the front door streetlight pours into the hall, sudden and scouring. The turbulence inside me is cold as the skin of frost on the pavement. I pass emaciated boys, drugged eyes flat as ironed sheets. I walk to the hospital gates then back past the mosque. Later there will be the call to prayer; elderly women will leave their houses in salwar kameez and flimsy footwear. Few believe they will stay long enough in this cold country to make use of a stout pair of shoes, or accept, even after forty years, that a temporary situation has become permanent.

I shall stay until Hasim comes. Where else in this big cooling world could he find me? If I walk far enough and check every face I shall recover him: my darling, my true love. Eight years have passed since the police took him away, but I shall recognise him. I spot him sometimes in a retreating back or a turned head. Once, outside the mosque in traditional dress. I had to smile - my atheist husband, are you really so changed? But close up just a boy, not like my Hasim at all.

One o'clock. I am tired now, sick with the thoughts of others. Seeking solace, clarity, in people's heads, I find only tracks in snow that loop and vanish. I do not know the reason for this malady, or the good of it. Perhaps one day meaning will come. But now I had better go home. Amos needs me; he cannot be left alone too long. I must hurry.

Curtin's Legacy

By Katherine Fay

Dad shot our sheep in the makeshift pen, dragged them into the pit and dropped them on top of each other. If their legs still kicked he put another bullet into them.

"Just nerves. It's dead, can't feel anything now." He explained this when I stared at the head and legs of the first sheep because they jerked like a broken robot, and after that I stopped worrying. I helped him to pull the animals from pen to pit. Whenever I tired of that my best friend Suzie Brady and I zig-zagged across the empty dam and threw at each other the jigsaw pieces that we peeled out of the cracked earth. Mid afternoon it grew so hot we scooped the mud from under these chunks of earth onto our cheeks and forehead.

"Mudmasks!" we yelled, waving from the dam bank at Dad as he walked to the pit to catch another sheep.

"D'you want one, John?" Suzie Brady said.

"Always very lady-like, aren't you two?" Dad had a habit of answering a question with another question. He squinted down at us when we reached him. The dust stuck to his face and made it even browner in the creases around his eyes and mouth.

"Can I've a go?" The loud cracking sound wasn't as shocking as usual. The shot went into the sheep's soft belly like a bullet into a pillow.

"Next time Jamie, never in the guts. Painful death. And slow." The older Dad got, the more he hated causing pain. The three of us stood and looked at the heaped bodies in the pit for a minute. The job was all finished but Dad didn't hum like he usually did when we closed the last gate or the woolshed door for the day. The sheep's eyes looked the same alive or dead.

"Can we've a Coke now, Dad?" I said, pulling at his hand. He walked back to the ute and placed the rifle behind the passenger seat. He turned to face me but he looked through us.

"Hm? Not today. C'mon."

"It's okay," Suzie Brady whispered and nudged me in the arm. "We've got Coke at our house."

We helped Dad dissemble the pen. Brown patches left a rough outline of where the little fences had been and the ground was stained for ages after. There was no grass and the dirt soaked the sheep blood right up. I think it was grateful for any kind of liquid.

"Shit."

I looked where Dad was looking. A lamb was in the next paddock and it seemed curious about us in the way that lambs do when they can't find their mothers anymore. Somehow in a summer full of dust its buzz-cut of a woollen coat had managed to stay a whitish shade. This one was different from our other lambs, the ones we'd loaded onto the truck three days earlier. Sheep were stupid, everyone knew that, but I loved lambs.

"Should we take it to the new farm where the others went so that it can have some hay too?" I asked.

"My Dad said when wool farmers put their sheep on trucks they're going straight to the dog food factory," said Suzie Brady. The Bradys had a few merinos but a lot more crops than sheep. They wore ironed shirts a lot, and Dad told me their farm was ten times the size of ours. I knew Meagan was wrong about the dog food because everything my Dad said turned out to be right. If he said there would be a north wind and a bad fire day, it came true. If he said Eagle Rock was next on the tape, he was right. Once we did an IQ test that was on TV and he scored one hundred and forty four. That was when I knew my Dad was not magical like I'd suspected, but almost a genius, like Einstein or like his hero John Curtin. I decided I would like John Curtin too when Dad told me that he was even his father's favourite politician. I never met my grandfather, but Dad told me little things about him. Like how he would spread the fleece over the woolshed floor and stay up until three a.m. picking the burrs and grass out. For his fleece he won an award which I kept on my cupboard. Dad didn't stay up until three a.m. and he threw the wool over a rotating table, not the floor, but I knew he worked very hard too because he sometimes fell asleep in the evenings in front of the ABC news.

"Bugger it." He shook his head and seemed angry at the lamb. Maybe he was annoyed because the lamb might have guessed its Mum was in the pit. He shook his head again and opened the driver's side door.

"You can't leave it there, it'll die!"

He frowned and half-moon lines appeared at the side of his mouth. I think he was too tired from the day's work to argue. "Catch it and you can keep it. But you feed it."

Before I killed the lamb, it nuzzled the rifle barrel.

"It thinks it's the bottle," I said. In the midst of my hysterics and hot angry tears I kept the gun pointed down at the lamb. "He looked so skinny! And I thought he was dying and I didn't know what to do!" My throat hurt from crying.

Dad held my arm steady.

"But it's cruel! You hate everyone, everything!"

Dad's face went red like he was holding his breath and his words came out in little explosions. "What's cruel is watching an animal starve to death. Waiting until it's too tired to keep the crows away and they pick out its eyes. That's cruelty. That's just weakness."

In the corner of the enclosure the food scraps were curled up and rotting, half covered in dust. I'd spent hours waving that food under the lamb's nose but it had ignored the treats and sucked my little finger instead. What it needed was Glycoside but the box was empty. I'd heard Mum and Dad arguing a week earlier and after that I knew I couldn't ask them to buy a new box. Dad had sounded angry when Mum said that maybe Liam Brady offering to buy us out wasn't such a bad thing. "It's been a bad year," said Dad, as if that settled the matter.

"John, what if next year's a bad one too?" she asked. I was not sure what would happen if next year was bad. I thought of playing on the haystack on our own farm with Suzie. "You can be first mate. It's my farm, so I'm captain," is what she would say. I decided to help Dad even more often than usual.

"Go on Jamie," he said. I shot that lamb and as I watched it die I started to hate my Dad.

My second visit home from uni was just before the start of my second year. It coincided with the worst bushfires in half a century. I put out the spotfires in our stubble and watched from the back of the truck as the trees in the next paddock grew orange billowing hair on top of their bodies that crackled and split. Neighbours said the sound was like a jet engine when the fire front swept over their houses. They crouched in their hallways with strips of wet cloth over their mouths. After the front passed they ran out outside and tried to put out the flames on their front doors, their rosebushes and their gutters with the black ground scorching their feet. From where we were poised, Dad in the cabin and four of us on the back peering out with stinging eyes, it was quieter than that. While my uni friends celebrated Australia Day on the St Kilda foreshore with casks and the Hottest 100, I was a black face in yellow overalls. Plumes of smoke encroached upon the cyan overhead. Licks of flame jumped on top of the eucalypts that stood at the end of the stretch of blonde stubble. It could have been a postcard: Australia, January. I felt more at home than I had in the last ten years, a large chunk of which I'd spent planning my escape from the place. I'd nagged about boarding school. When that had failed I'd studied harder than the other kids at my country high school. If somebody asked me what I wanted to do after school, my answer was always, "I want to go to uni in the city."

We sat on the back porch steps and drank Crownies. I got the impression Dad was pleased to have me home, even though he'd lost three hundred ewes that day. He was the man I remembered from when I was a little kid, the one who always took a second before answering. The one who called Hungry Jack's 'Hopeless Joe's' to my shrieks of laughter and who lamented the demise of the Sunday mass as the regional catch-up session of his parent's era, even though he rarely bothered going.

"When are you going back?" he said.

"Tomorrow."

He finished the last of his bottle. "Could use you on the truck again. Still burning over the far west corner of Brady's."

"I'll see."

"Goodnight." He patted me on the head.

The rains later that night meant most of the volunteers were stood down. In the morning Dad and I picked up the dead sheep using a loader. Sometimes the prongs speared the bloated bellies and popped the carcass. There was lots of dripping. "I'm never eating meat again," I said at least five times. That afternoon we fenced at a burned-out neighbour's property switching the radio from ABC National to JJJ and back whenever one noticed the other had changed it. In the evening we watched the newsreaders gush about politician visits and CFA heroes while the camera panned out around the charred hills and houses.

"Suzie said they buried two thousand today in total. Her place and MacDougalls," I said, still watching the news.

"Bet the honourable local member wasn't out there with her. Too busy smiling for the camera," said Dad. We heard a vehicle pull up. Liam Brady knocked and at the same time pushed the screen door open. He did it in the way that people who don't really need to knock do it out of politeness.

"G'day, Liam. Suzie."

"John, Jamie. Picked up a few today?"

"About three hundred. We were lucky. Jamie said you guys had a couple of thousand. Drink?"

"No thanks. Got to get home. Whole lot of burned ones waiting in the sheds. MacDougalls're worse off. Still another day's worth of dead ones there."

"Need a hand?"

"Yeah, thanks..Yeah. Just can't do any more. Can't shoot any more of my own."

Mum walked in. "Cup of tea, Liam? Hello, Suzie. How'd netball go last weekend?" Liam looked at Mum a moment.

"C'mon. Stay here, have a drink." I patted Dad on his balding head. "Suze and I'll do it. You men are getting soft in your old age."

"If their noses or feet are black, you've just got to shoot them. How's uni?"

"Fine. Fun. It's weird though, it's really nice to be home." Suzie reloaded and I dragged another one up the ramp into the back of the truck.

"Do you mind? This?"

"What?" she said. "Shooting them? No." She shrugged. "They're insured. Everyone around here's insured. Not really fun though, is it?"

"Let me have a go." I was surprised to feel a little repulsed each time I pulled the trigger. I couldn't tell the difference between weakness and compassion anymore.

"What'll happen, do you reckon?" We looked at each other: dirty faces, blood on our clothes, shooting our fathers' livestock. I saw an image of us in ten years time in the same clothes covered in the same ash and dust. "Are you ever leaving?"

"Nope. Not yet. I'm happy here." I envied her certainty. Dad had never taught me how to leave.

"Let's drive past the pit on the way home," I said. I wanted to know if the bloodstains had washed away.

Do I Hear Seven Hundred and Fifty?
(Honorable Mention)

By Mark Fink

As a jackhammer pounded in my head and the pungent taste of liquor rushed its way up my throat, I tried to sit up and blink my eyes into focus. It would be nice if I could also remember my name and where the hell I was. Scanning the room, it looked vaguely familiar: gaudy wallpaper, tacky plastic fixtures burning sixty watt bulbs, and an ancient fifteen inch TV which sat atop a tower of dresser drawers. I was in a cheap motel.

I heard a toilet flush followed by not so dainty footsteps. A statuesque woman appeared naked before me. She winked and it all started coming back. This was my date for the evening. As she limped across the lime green carpet, every joint in her body snapped, crackled and popped. I guess that's what you get when you date a professional wrestler, one who's broken thirteen bones. She was not anywhere near my type, but this was not anywhere near an ordinary evening.

It all began innocently enough six hours earlier. As the weekday weatherman for channel eight, I attended the station's annual charity ball, where, along with the rest of the news team, I was put up for auction. Some lucky bidder would get to have me to herself for one night, which, if you asked any of the six women I had dated up to that point, was not something on which to squander one's hard-earned money. Our obnoxious Ken Doll anchorman sold for thirty-two hundred dollars to some socialite with a serious overbite. Talk about money down the drain. The man is a total nitwit and I'm not just saying that because he makes five times what I do and is dating one of the Desperate Housewives.

My name was called and I walked onto the stage trying to fake a sincere smile. Men going to the electric chair have shown more enthusiasm. As I did the obligatory 360-degree turn to give everyone the best view of the merchandise, I once again deeply regretted dropping out of pharmacy school. To my amazement, the bidding was brisk and spirited. After several bids that pushed my price north of four hundred, it came down to two final pursuers. One was a very pleasant looking lady in her mid-thirties with an engaging smile who looked like she not only read but subscribed to *The New Yorker*. Just the type of woman I've been dying to meet. The other was something quite different. She looked very large, even sitting in her chair. She was poured into a flaming red cocktail dress that was cut so low, not one, but two waiters had dropped trays of champagne as they walked one way and gawked another.

As the bidding escalated I tried desperately to send some kind of signal to Ms. New Yorker, pleading with a wink that screamed "Buy me!" But I never could wink and my wink turned into a hideous eye twitch. Ms. New Yorker abruptly stopped the bidding at $650 and bolted for the bar. She was either very turned off or very thirsty. The Amazon in the red dress apparently got off on my twitching and promptly bid me up to $700. The gavel pounded and I was hers.

She introduced herself as Debbie Duncan but said I probably knew her as Demolition Debbie, her wrestling stage name. I didn't. Debbie explained that she had made a nice living but was now on the shelf thanks to a ruptured spleen, courtesy of a male wrestler who threw her out of the ring into the fourth row.

"I'm back to hating men," she informed me. "Does next Saturday work for you?"

She took me to a downtown dive bar where the clientele looked so scary, I was actually relieved to be with someone who could break a man's neck with a simple twist. Debbie insisted I order something called The Kamikaze. This wasn't a drink, it was Alzheimer's in a glass. After three sips I started singing the score to Cabaret. Debbie ordered up another round and gave me an oral history of her wrestling injuries. The poor girl had broken both arms, both kneecaps, eight fingers, and dislocated pretty much of everything else. But the one that stood out was the thirty-six stitches on her left buttock sustained when she wrestled an alligator and came in second. Having downed my second Kamikaze like it was lemonade, I felt bold enough to tell her about my battle scar. I rolled up my pants and proudly displayed the two-inch jagged line on my left shin. Had I been thinking clearly, I would have said it was the result of a knife fight, or at least an injury from some football game from my glory days. But after a second tumbler of truth serum I felt compelled to share how Rabbi Bluestein dropped the Torah on my leg during my Bar Mitzvah reading. When she stopped laughing Debbie turned to me with a look of resignation. "You're my first Jew."

"Well, that makes us even. You're my first wrestler."

She pulled her chair closer and smiled, revealing a set of dentures that could only have been purchased in a strip mall.

"I have a confession to make. I watch you do the weather every night at eleven."

"Thank you. My mother watches at eleven."

"And when I watch. . . I touch myself."

"Oh. I don't think Mom does that."

"Let's get out of here, stud."

So, that's how I ended up in room 111 of the Kiss 'N Tell Motor Court. Debbie stood before me in all her splendor. She was some specimen: six foot two, two hundred and twenty pounds, three percent body fat. I was dating an NFL linebacker who just happened to have a vagina. I sat up in bed and realized for the first time that I was naked as well. Built more like an NFL ticket taker, I'm uncomfortable even undressing in front of myself. I reflexively pulled the sheet over my lap.

"Dude," she said, "It's a little late for that." That's when it dawned on me.

"Debbie, did we . . you know."

"Fuck? I did my best, but you passed out stud. And just for the record, you've got like the smallest dick I've ever seen."

There was a confidence builder. "Well, would you look at the time? I better get going-early day tomorrow."

"Early day my ass," she snapped. "You're on at four, six and eleven, weather boy. You probably don't even get up 'til noon. Hey, I paid seven hundred bucks for you and I'm going to get my money's worth." With that, she took out a pair of handcuffs.

Me and my small penis sensed trouble. Maybe it was the handcuffs or maybe the mere fact that she could bench press a washer-dryer, but my utterly incomplete life flashed before my eyes. I could see the story on Entertainment Tonight: WEATHERMAN SNUFFED OUT IN TAWDRY SEXCAPADE. Who was I kidding; I'd never make Entertainment Tonight. I took another look at the handcuffs and for the first time that evening, started to think clearly.

"I've really got to pee."

"Well hurry up, weather boy, I've got big plans for you."

I scurried to the bathroom, locked the door and turned on the water. The window. It was my only hope. Fueled by adrenaline and pure fear, I was no longer Weatherman; I was now a superhero: Naked Man. I hoisted myself up to the sliding window and contorted my body through the two-foot opening. Sometimes a small penis can be your best friend. As Debbie called for me again, I took a flying leap toward the balcony railing, grabbed it and swung myself like a monkey onto the patio of the adjacent motel room. Landing on my back, the pain was almost unbearable, but that was the easy part. Drapes parted and two white-haired ladies stared down at me, enjoying the view.

"Isn't that the weather guy from channel eight?"

"Yes. And he looks so much smaller in person."

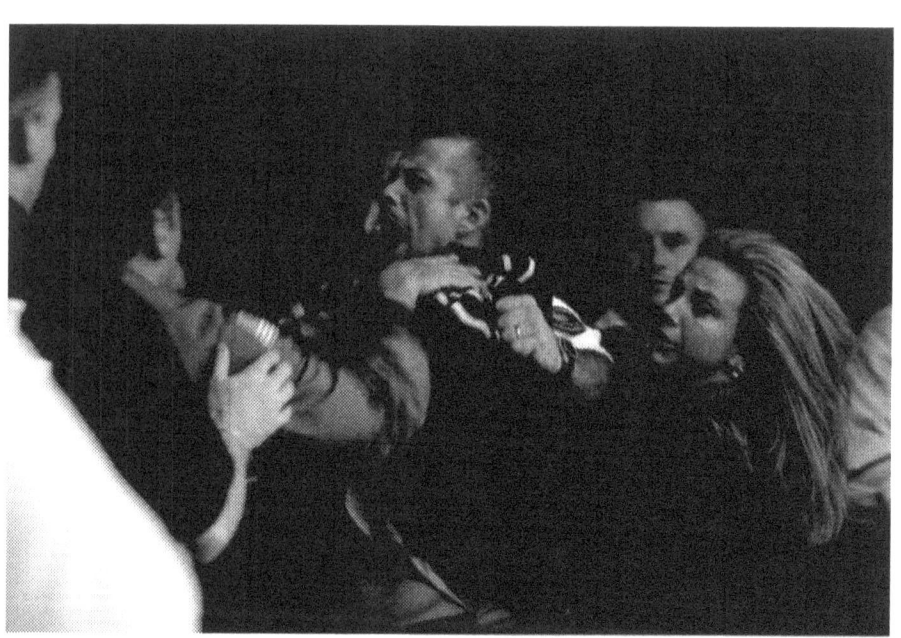

Plan B

By David Fulton

My mother used to say: "Don't leave those big knives lying around, you never know." But she never finished the sentence. I asked her over and over again what she meant by "You never know," but she always brushed me off with "Oh, it doesn't matter".

That was all I could think of the whole night long. And it was a long night. First came the neighbours crowding up the narrow staircase and all cramped in together like sardines in a little can. Then came the local police, two of them with their big black truncheons and looking as if they meant business as they pushed their way through the tight-packed sardines until they got to the front door yelling at the neighbours to stand back.

I knew what the police meant when they said "Stand back" because they said the same thing the last time they came and there were just as many sticky-beak neighbours on that occasion.

It wasn't that those neighbours came to help. They just wanted to know what was going on and get to see themselves on the late-night television news. The television news was sure to be there because they follow the police around like bees to a honey-pot. They can smell trouble a mile off and our staircase was always a trouble-spot. You could always find some juicy bit of news right on our own doorstep. You didn't have to go to the Gaza Strip or Baghdad or Afghanistan. It was right there for the camera crew to film before the police arrived.

But this time, the police beat them to it and the neighbours were muttering among themselves saying they should put them all in jail if they even came anywhere near their wives when there was an order out saying to keep away or else they'd be breaking Article 131, Clause 17. That's where it said everything in all that legal language nobody could understand unless you were a high-priced lawyer or something like that, which I wasn't, nor any of the neighbours who were simple folk just like us who had to go to work to get money to buy food, if there was any work, that is, which usually there wasn't.

Within a few seconds that seemed like hours to me the police were right at the front door mat and banging on the door and shouting "Police here, open up!" That's what they always said: "Police here, open up!" To me, it seemed a pretty stupid thing for them to say because in our house, if anyone yelled out "Police here, open up!", the last thing anyone thought of doing was opening that door. While the police were waiting a few seconds for someone to open the door, this always allowed the "culprit" to put Plan B into action.

The "culprit" was my own father and, for the seventh or eighth time, he had done what he wasn't supposed to do. He'd broken Article 131, Clause 17 or whatever it was he was not supposed to break and he'd come home. Well, it wasn't really his home any more but I guess I wanted him to come home and be my father and love my mother and my little sister and just like being with all of us and wanting to be there and act sweet and loving and cracking jokes like he used to do with me and my sister and even with my mother a long time ago.

My father was no dummy. If he came home and he wasn't supposed to come anywhere near my mother, he always had an escape plan ready to put into action at a moment's notice. If you're doing something you're not supposed to be doing, like robbing a bank, you have to have a Plan B just in case anything goes wrong. It's something my father said he learned in the army. They always had to have Plan B ready just in case the enemy came from the opposite direction or did something else unexpected.

Plan B was your escape plan. You had to have Plan B properly worked out, of course, so you knew all the details ahead of time and could put it into practice at any moment without a second's delay otherwise it could mean the end of you.

In my father's case, Plan B, at home not in the army, was worked out to the ultimate degree. It took five seconds to carry it out and it was so simple it was practically fool-proof. It was the five seconds between when the police called out "Police here, open up" and when they broke down the door that really mattered. Sometimes I wondered if my father had had a kind of Plan B worked out from when he was a kid, a kind of lifetime Plan B for keeping out of trouble or, if he got into trouble, for getting out of it in five seconds flat.

He must have had a plan like that from when he was a kid or he wouldn't have always been getting into so much trouble and then getting out of so much trouble afterwards. My father was as quick as a mountain goat and he could climb up a drain-pipe or slither down one while most other people would be wondering where to find a ladder or a rope that would reach that far.

My father's Plan B when he came home when he shouldn't have was simple. He would climb out onto the bricks just outside the kitchen window quick as a flash and slither down the drain-pipe to the back porch of the neighbour's house. That took about four seconds. This left him all of one second to jump onto of a shelf on the neighbour's level and hide before the police burst into our house with their pistols drawn and yelling out "Police here, come out with your hands up!"

My mother always came out with her hands up, at least with one hand up because she was carrying my little sister in the other. She always called out first "Don't shoot, he isn't here!" She was telling the honest truth because, thanks to Plan B, my father was already well hidden and out of harm's way.

Of course, the police would then search the house and look under the beds and open all the cupboards. They never found him, of course, because of Plan B. And my mother would beg the police to go and send all the neighbours away because there was nothing to worry about and she was not in any danger. No, she hadn't seen her husband that day or yesterday or last week. He was under an order not to come near the house and that was that. One of the police would always try to be nice and friendly and say: "Look, if you have any problems, just call us. That's what we're here for. And keep in touch with your neighbours. They're only trying to help".

That was how Plan B had worked for at least ten times or even more. It was hard to keep count because it had happened so many times. No one should have to remember things they don't want to remember. I didn't want to go over all those times even once more. It's like putting your brain through a mincing machine to squeeze out all the real facts and the possible facts and the whys and the wherefores and the whos and the whats and the dates no one would ever want to remember ever again in one's whole lifetime.

Who would want to keep in their brain the date your own father last beat your mother with a rolling pin and broke her arm in three places and left her lying unconscious on the living-room floor? I wanted to wipe it all right out of my mind for ever, to make it a great big blank of a date on the calendar, a day that never took place, a day when the sun didn't even rise or set, when everything that day was as black as night so that it wasn't really a day at all but a big dark circle around both my eyes that blotted out my memory of that awful time.

That was how I always felt but deep down, I suppose, I had something of my mother's eternal hope that one day my father would really straighten out and finally come to his senses and decide that, after all, he did love us and wanted to give us all his love and look after us and have fun with us and make jokes like he used to do. I know I said that before but when you want something really badly you keep saying the same thing over and over again in the hope that if you say it often enough it will really come true. Now I wish I had said all those things over and over again a lot more.

I tried that for a long time. I tried it every time my father came home when he was not supposed to come home. The trouble was he'd start off all right and everything would be fine. He'd be nice to my mother and to us kids and he'd either bring us fancy presents or he'd promise to buy us all sorts of things we knew he couldn't afford and for a while things looked as if he were going to stay and that everything bad that had happened before would be put in the past and buried and forgotten forever and that my mother would be smiling and happy again and that my little sister would be laughing all the time and that my father would be making all his old jokes again and we'd be just a normal family like all the others in the building.

It was going to be the beginning of a new life and the sun and the moon and the stars would all be glittering and the birds in the trees would be singing and the neighbour's dog would barking just because it liked to bark. Nobody could have been happier than me if it had only lasted even one long wonderful day. But it never did. Something always happened to change things around, to make the sun dark and the stars lose their sparkle, to stop the birds from singing and to put an end to the happy barking of our neighbour's dog.

What was it that made everything change? I could never really find out. But something always did happen to make the day turn sour. Could it have been something I said or the way I looked when my father spoke or could I have looked at my little sister at the wrong moment or could I have hugged my mother when I should have been doing something else? All of those things went spinning through my head and a thousand other crazy thoughts as well as I tried to sift through the thoughts, the words, the actions, the mistakes I might have made that day, a day when I needed to have done everything just perfectly, to have spoken with the greatest love and affection, or acted in the most tender possible way toward my father.

I wanted my father back at all costs. And it didn't seem such a lot to pay. I was ready to be loving to him. I was ready to be warm. I was ready to laugh at all his crazy old jokes. I was ready to be the apple of his eye, or anything else, if that would bring him back as my father who loved me and wanted to hug me and kiss me and just be my really own father.

When I look back now I know I had pushed my way to front door just as the police were knocking hard with their truncheons and calling out "Police here, open up!" And they smashed down the door just like that. There was no time for Plan B that day. I keep wishing my father had got away just like he'd done so many times before but wishing is not going to change a thing. It never does. The trouble is I don't know what really happened in those last precious five seconds. I was out on the staircase with all the sticky-beak neighbours and the police yelling and banging on the door and I was just coming home from school and I didn't even know my father was there with my mother and my little sister.

If I try to put the pieces together the problem is they don't all fit like a nice neat puzzle. My father used to do puzzles with me so I know all about puzzles and I used to be pretty good at doing them. My father was quick but I often used to be even faster. Sometimes he used to get angry if I found a piece faster than he did. In fact, once he went almost crazy and threw the whole puzzle in the fireplace where we had a roaring fire going and you could tell he was very, very angry because his face was all screwed up and he kept repeating words I didn't understand at the time, like "Ne'er-do-well" or something like that. He was so angry I was quite scared and I wanted to run to my mother but I tried to calm him down and I threw my arms around his leg and squeezed but he pushed me away as if he didn't want anyone to touch him. As I say, all the pieces don't really fit together. Something must have gone wrong with Plan B or he must have gone crazy like he did with that puzzle.

When the police finally got into the living room, there was my mother lying on the floor all covered with blood, and my little sister too, and there was my father with a big knife in his hand and he was on the floor too all covered with blood. I immediately thought of my mother and how she used to say: "Don't leave those big knives lying around, you never know."

It was a long night with the police and neighbours and everyone asking me questions, questions and more questions. I couldn't find any answers, of course. How could I have any answers? If I'd had any answers none of this would have happened and we'd all be together living like all the other families in the building. I'd be doing puzzles with my father again. I knew all about Article 131, Clause 17 or whatever it was but I desperately wanted my father to come home. I wish he'd stuck to Plan B.

For Rany

By Babette Gallard

"Pick a time. Pick a place."

"What time? What place?"

"Anywhere you'd like to be right now."

"Somewhere I've already been?"

"It's up to you."

Maybe it's something to do with the greyness of the light; the monochrome before evening finally shifts into night. Or maybe it's just because this is the only time of the day when they can be alone together, but they always start talking at about this time.

Talking is easier when no one else is around, but the house always seems to be full of people. He's never had so many friends.

People dropping by to say "Hi, how you doing Chris? You're looking good."

People who whisper in the next room that it's a shame for someone so young. People he hardly knew before.

The nurse, even though there's nothing left for her to do, because Kate has being doing it for weeks; the patting and the pulling and the draining and the wiping. Dealing with the most private parts of him and stripping away any pretence or dignity. They've each accepted it now, but he remembers when it wasn't so easy.

"I can do it myself. Anyway you hurt because you don't know how."

"The nurse showed me how, Chris."

"The nurse showed me how, Chris." Since when did he start doing impersonations?

"Come on. Think of a place, any place, and describe it."

"Can I take you with me?"

"If you want, but it's your dream and I won't be hurt if you say you want to go alone."

It used to hurt. At the beginning, when he didn't know what it was, it hurt even more. When he felt the pain building up he used to pretend he was sneaking out for a smoke, even though he'd given up years ago.

Kate got upset and they argued, but arguing was easier than talking about how it felt to be pissing broken glass.

"Why start smoking now?" She used to shout at him. "After all this time and when you're playing rugby every weekend and doing all that circuit training? It's crazy. No, it's worse than that it's just bloody stupid. Do you want me to remind you of the way my sister died? Is that the way you want to go too?"

But all the time he was going anyway.

When the results came through, he'd shouted at her as if she was to blame for what the doctor had just told them.

"I know I've been selfish and I've got a long list of apologies to make, but am I that bad? Can anyone be bad enough to deserve this?"

She'd kissed him then, her lips hot and uncertain, whispering that only people who believed in a divine being could believe in divine retribution. So that was that, he didn't believe in a god so he could only put it down to bastard bad luck.

When he told his parents, his Mum said it was the food they ate and the water they drank and the air they breathed. Then she'd started crying, a kitten sound moaned into her hands with his Dad collapsed around her so that together they reminded him of a Rodin sculpture.

"Have you thought of anything yet?"

Her face is in shadow, but a sliver of light is highlighting the soft hairs on her chin. He tries to imagine her older, the hairs hardened to pert bristles that she'll pluck covertly like his Mum.

"I've got them on my nipples too." She'd told him when he'd caught her in the bathroom once. "It comes with age. Men get balder and we get hairier. A design fault. One of many."

He'd felt sorry for her then and noticed for the first time that she'd stopped wearing makeup and painting her nails.

Kate's hands aren't like his Mum's. They're rough and gritty. It's what he'd liked about her from the start. Her difference. He looks at her again and it's as if with the darkening room a light is going on in his own head.

"I'm thinking back."

The streets lights have come on, slicing the room into slabs of black and white and turning his tears into silver trails that run down the sides of his eyes and into his hair.

"Listen to me Kate. Tell me you understand. I can't get it up. I can't pee and when I do pee, I pee blood. I hate every minute of every day. I want it to stop, but then I don't, because it will be forever."

"No, only we can be forever. You said you were thinking back. Paint the picture for me."

He feels her body moving over his skin as she checks the tubes and monitors his temperature with her lips. Does she regret that everything she has learnt will be wasted? Will she sculpt emaciated bodies and death when it's all over? He doesn't want to ask. His hand is clammy and the sweat dribbling off his top lip is bitter on his tongue.

"How can I paint a smell? The smell of warm bodies in the sun."

"Where are you?"

"On a beach. We went one summer, I think it was Spain. I'm lying on Mum, her belly soft and her tits are falling out at the sides of her costume. Dad's smiling and I can see the leftover of a chocolate ice cream stuck on the front tooth that's whiter than the rest. It's a crown but I didn't know that then."

"How old are you?"

"Nine maybe ten." I don't know why, but lying on her has given me a hard-on and I'm embarrassed.

Then Mum says. "Keep that for your other women, young man."

And Dad says, "Son, there's a name for that kind of thing."

I ask him what it is, but he just laughs and then we all laugh. That's what I remember most, the laughing.

"Is that your place?"

"Getting there."

He has closed his eyes, but he sees and feels and smells it all as if he were there right now, outside in the cold air. November and his feet are freezing. He's walked in through the blue door that's metal with reinforced glass windows in it. Institutional. Ugly.

"Don't leave me alone. Tell me what you're seeing." Her eyes are searching his as if the picture was in the black pupils.

"Not seeing, smelling. Why is it that the smell always comes first?"

"It's our most primordial sense, the one that saved us from Mammoths and Sabre Toothed tigers."

"But it's not just a smell; it's more a dampness in the air, the sort that seeps in through brick. You were wearing those fingerless gloves that first time, and when you shook my hand it felt like holding icicles."

"The pipes had blown that morning. Don't you remember me telling you?"

"I'd come to look at the studios to get an idea of what was needed for the renovation project. My first job."

"You hadn't got a clue."

"You said so."

"Did I?"

"The clay was everywhere, in bags, in lumps, in streaks across the wall. You told me your day job was teaching disturbed teenagers and you showed me some of their work. Gross, twisted, filthy stuff, but I tried to say the right things. Then you showed me the drawings of what you thought the centre should look like and I felt like packing up and going home because they were better than anything I could have done."

"You didn't tell me."

There's a lot he hasn't told her, because before he'd always thought it could wait and now he doesn't want to. A tremor flickers in the fingers of his hand, cupped round her warm breast, inside the T-shirt that's still got paint on the sleeve from when they decorated the kitchen; a bright red scuff matching the wall he can see through the half open door.

"I'm in the place." He says.

"Where?"

"Next to the kiln and the shelves where you kept the stuff made by your students. I'm standing in front of the cupboard, the one with the glass door."

"Where I kept my own work?"

"Yeh, the bronze casts of your clay figures. Do you remember how I recognized one of them?"

"Tell me."

He smiles because they both know the words, but she wants to hear him say them.

"Me: Did you do that?

You: Yes, it's what I do.

Me: But that's our trophy.

You: Do you play for the Exiles then?

Me: I'm Captain. We won it this year.

You: And I made it."

Now he sees bronze figure again. A rugby player caught in mid-flight, the power of a young, muscular man in shorts.

He has the feeling still, burning through him just as it did when he ran for the line. The thrill and pain held like a nut within the core of the metal, bursting for the leap and bunching on the fall. Rocks on rocks.

"Lie still," she says. "I'll be back."

A car slows down to park outside in the street below. Two doors open and close. A man coughs. Probably the new couple from downstairs. Cindy Briars is walking her dog on her too-high heels, just as she will tomorrow and the day after and the day after that, until one day she won't anymore, but there will always be a car door slamming and a woman walking her dog, tip-tapping, for someone else to hear.

He calls out. "Will you keep my jacket Kate? The leather one. Will you wear it?"

"Yes and I'll sleep in your T-shirts."

She comes back in and turns on the small table lamp in the corner. It gives out an orange glow that makes the sickly yellow of his arms sulphurous. They are soft and hairless and his flesh hangs on his body as if it should belong to someone much larger.

"I don't want you to remember me like this."

But she will remember everything. Her eyes bright as she closes his fingers round the bronze figure, curling his palm so that he can feel the tension of the muscles again, the jumping before the falling. Rocks on Rocks. Then a small twist of pain as the needle pierces his skin.

"You'll sleep." She whispers, her breath warm on his cheek and her body taking the shape of his own where she lies beside him. "Then it will be dawn."

"And what will you do?"

"I'll get up and wear your jacket and smell your smell and carry you in the palm of my hand."

"And I'll be there forever."

Passport

By Jennifer Hill

"You keep that up, mister, and when we get home, I get out the spoon." His little tow head is a beacon of light above his face, crumpled and red; thick, clear boogies run down his nose into his lips. He cries with his mouth closed. Two-and-a-half. Maybe three. She is stern and slender, except for a pudge around her middle. Her older boy stands by, knowingly, watching little brother cry it out. They both believe her about the spoon: one from experience, one from fear. She is a normal woman, but about thirty of us are paying attention without looking, judging her a terrible mother.

BWI is thick with impatient travellers waiting for luggage. The bitch who sat next to me on the plane stands thinly near the waving strips, wafting, covering the luggage portal, behind which our bags are hefted onto the belt with no ceremony and less care. Mine comes out nearly first, and I lug it waiting for the shuttle, through the garage, both hot, sticky, and pay fifty-five cash for the week. I get on 195 thinking about the little boy, wondering if she will beat him with the spoon when they get home. He didn't look like he was near done crying.

My apartment – a house, really; I have the whole thing, semi-detached with garage – is cool and smells like the inside of a plastic bag. I flip on the light and drop my overstuffed bag in the hallway. I just make it to the toilet. Ahh. Travel is for other people. I pile dirty clothes into the washer, leave the fresh in the suitcase, put the duty free in the liquor cabinet, and pad to the refrigerator. My week-old iced coffee in its stained Tupperware pitcher looks good, but it's after 10 p.m. and I would never sleep. Reynardo is coming tomorrow, for the garage door, at 8 a.m. Or is that next week? I am too tired to find my calendar and check it. I reach for a yogurt, expired, but confident that they take at least another month to go bad, I climb the stairs with it. I think for the thousandth time, screw the landlord I will get a dog, as I sink into my too-hard bed, the one that was supposed to be a pillow-top, that I needed on delivery, and couldn't send back to get the right one. I couldn't be uncomfortable for one night without a mattress, so now I'm uncomfortable every night with this one. My sheets are soft. They smell like me. I should bottle it and sell it: Spinster. Terrible idea. Stop being so negative.

I am so afraid of the sounds at night and this one is no different. Probably the screen door loose again, but I am too afraid to go down. I bury my head under the covers and pretend I didn't hear it, wish again, pray again, that God will send me a man who doesn't think I'm too depressed or too fat or too loud or too happy in the lee of his kindness, and that I will one day sleep next to someone who isn't afraid to get up and check the screen door, to have a little tow-headed boy with, whom we would never beat with a spoon. The hand on my ankle is cold and I am too frightened to scream. The bedcovers come off and I am embarrassed that I fell asleep with the half-eaten yogurt on the covers. I notice the smudge of the rest of it on the wall. The smudge fascinates me while he pulls my T-shirt off, rips it. It hurts on my neck where it rips. I should be screaming, but I am so afraid. Or I am trying to, but the scream won't come out. I don't know whether to look or not to look. I don't know what to do, and then it's over and I see something glinting. A knife. That is what must have hurt on my neck, not the T-shirt ripping. There is no face, just a knife and a smell like grease or oil, like from a car exhaust. I don't know what color or size. I don't know what to do, so I lie there, wondering if I will die.

The light through the window shutters is watery and clear. It ripples over the sheets, bright enough to see the room, but not to show the blood and shit stains that I can smell now. I am not dead. I wiggle my toes and they wiggle and I want to cry like the boy with the spoon, but I can't. I close my eyes and try to will sleep. Instead, my tongue worries the gritty blood on my lips, where I bit, or he, and I don't sleep. I pretend to sleep. I try to think of something nice, but keep picturing the yogurt hitting the wall, keep hearing the spoon clatter on my wide-plank wood floors, refurbished by the landlord, to further lure me into paying too much rent in this safe, landmark neighborhood. I should be in a complex with a pool and a doorman. But I wanted wide-plank floors, high ceilings, and a covered porch with a screen door; my country girl oasis in the city, my Homeland. Maybe if I lie here long enough, I will bleed out, like on ER.

I call in sick very late, too late, at 12:30 p.m. They are angry and don't believe I have a cold. I put my comforter and sheets and spoon and yogurt cup and ripped T-shirt in a garbage bag on the back porch. DNA. Wednesday is recycling. Thursday is trash. Today is Monday. Bottles and cans. I am cold. I watch the food shows. My toes are very cold. I turn up the cooking shows and leave the bathroom door open and get in the tub. I try, but I have to breathe, so I just sit there, scalding. If I had a dog, I would name him Buddy. I sit in the tub yelling, "Here, Buddy!" over and over. I think I am yelling, but I cannot hear myself. I pour the rest of the bleach and the hydrogen peroxide in the scalding water and try again, but still I cannot and have to breathe. I get up. There are no clean towels. Soaking wet I put on my sweatsuit and go down to the kitchen. I want my iced coffee but don't want it to be a memory of this, so I have the soy milk instead. I want peanut butter but don't want it to be a memory of this, so I have the yogurt instead. Three more left. I eat them all because I will never eat it again. I try to cry but the sweatsuit is too bulky and wet and presses my lungs down so I go back to the bathroom and look through all the prescriptions again. Clindamycin, Doryx, folic acid. I don't lead the Xanax Valium Nebutol life. I could have too-clear skin, that's the most forgetting I can do in a bottle. I call 911.

"I was raped last night." They want my name and number, but that's all I can say. I hang up quickly, worried that they will trace the call. I remember that there are dark-chocolate covered raspberry jelly candies in the pantry. I sit on the pantry floor and eat them all. When I'm done, the doorbell rings. Officer Perkins.

He is twenty-six or twenty-seven. I don't let him in, but the doors are all open, that must be why I'm cold, and he is in the living room not touching anything, not moving, asking if he can help me, asking me my name, if I can see his fingers and if I have any pain. I keep walking backwards further into the pantry, even though I am sitting down, but there is no more room here. He moves to touch me and I wake up in dry itchy skin, there are lights above me and I must be in a hospital, except it is moving. Ambulance. Officer Perkins is gone and I am moved under light and cold and then I'm under an Indian man with very long nose hairs over his mask who is talking through it to me about how he has to do this and that and it will just hurt a bit. I wonder what is left to take. They want the number of someone to call. I try to tell them no, but there is a bag over my head-no, over my mouth. It's not enough to stop the breathing, either, even though it hurts. I feel water in my ears. I must be crying. Then I'm under light and cold again, unseasonably cold for June, amazing really, how cold it is, and then the scary one looks down at me, from higher above, her face distorted in her reflection in the curving metal light, like those timpani drums, above. Dishwater hair, face pale and lopsided like in a fun-house mirror, big purplish freckles on her neck that blend together in a line. She is talking, but her lips are barely moving, so I have no idea what she's saying to them, answering their questions to me. Strange, the safety in her gaze, which also scares the shit out of me. They wipe it up and she watches from the aluminum funhouse light, fascinated, devoid of manners.

The nurses are ashamed to be in the room with me. It is the second day and I want to get out of here except it means going home and I don't want to go there. The lady from Social Services comes and I tell her to sell everything in my apartment. She says no. On day five, I leave in my sweatsuit and check into the Ramada on York Road. I call some realtor in Towson out of the book and pretend I live out of state and that I'm my sister and my sister has died. They don't believe me. I call another one in Stoneleigh and then another in Govans. I say I need someone to clear everything out and sell it and send me a money order at the Ramada. They say no. Not they, Betty: Fifty-something, smoker, probably the receptionist, probably overweight, working in Govans but probably living in Loch Raven.

"Betty, I would of course expect you to keep thirty percent of the total sale, as your fee."

"Forty."

I Fed/Ex her the keys. Five days later, miraculously, Betty calls back. They are in a little lot behind Old York Road, behind a bridal shop; I ask the cabbie to wait. I give my name to the receptionist and she-it's Betty, her hands are very pale and smooth on the bottom, but wrinkled caramel on top-hands me a thick brown envelope. The hands say she's more like sixty than fifty. I can't look at her eyes and they are politely permitting me not to. I wait until I get back to the Ramada to open it, but ask the cabbie to wait. $4,916 in cash. Staggering, but then I remember my grandmother's Limoges, the Shaker sideboard, the rest of it, three floors, the car. Staggering; Betty could have done a lot with this. I try to understand how she didn't, or that she did, and why she called, but the thoughts are too heavy and I let them drop, all that I can understand about Betty is her hands, her polite brown eyes, her smell of paper and ink and coffee and the envelope in my hands.

I go back down to the cabbie who takes me to a check cashing place. "Which one, miss?"

"Any one."

"Tell me please where to go, please, miss."

"Any one. There must be one on one of these streets. The first one we see."

He takes me further down York, and I pay a $36.78 fee to cash out my checking account. I hold the thick envelope, thicker now, in my hands. Betty had some sort of homemade stew or chili on her desk, something musky, sweet. It stained the envelope. Officer Perkins must have put my bag in the ambulance. He said he had found it in the hall where I left it, oddly untouched. I keep only the government-issue IDs (state, Social Security, passport) because I have to, but bend and rip and throw everything else into the check-cashing-place trash. Just the IDs and the envelope go back in. My cabbie takes me toward the airport, he is my cabbie now, there is glass that separates us and he talks through the money hole, keeping the partition closed, like I want; even though I don't tell him to do so, he can tell. We stop at a strip mall next and I go into a sports store and buy a new sweatsuit while he idles. I buy a fanny pack. A pink leather one with a feather on the zipper. The sweatsuit is sapphire blue velour. I buy white sneakers with a hot pink stripe. I buy the thickest pair of socks I can find that are sold just as one pair and not twelve. I buy a white sport's bra that is so big it looks like a straight jacket. They don't sell underwear, so I buy thick white cotton bike shorts that are so small they should be underwear. I pay cash and change in the dressing room. I think to leave the clothes there, but don't want to alert the sports store people. I throw them out in the strip mall garbage instead, thinking why would they be alerted, and to what, how stupid. And then Djubani my driver, takes me to the airport and I buy a ticket to Shannon. It's nine hours plus, including the jump to Dublin. I do what I always do on planes, imagine and attend my death and wonder who would notice. Work. Landlord. Betty? No. Djubani? No. Jeremy from next door who mows the lawn and rakes the leaves will feel cheated when it's time to pick up his pay. My brother in Tucson calls every Easter and every Thanksgiving, so there is plenty of time without worrying about that. Mutual funds, 401(k), cable, phone, Omaha steaks, there is time, some other time. I arrive and take a taxi cab.

"Downtown, please."

"Hotel, miss?"

"No, just downtown. A pub."

"Which one, miss?"

"Not the famous one. Another one."

"Which one?"

"Any one."

I sit at the bar and let the first boy named Danny who wants to, kiss me. He takes me back to his apartment, which he calls flat, and we have sex without a condom. He doesn't know what to do with me. I say I am on vacation and always wanted to see Dublin. I say a lot of lies, and I am fine. I am bright but quiet in my blue sweatsuit and Danny likes the way I lie there and don't do anything while he does whatever he wants. Sometimes for just a few minutes, sometimes for longer. His skin is white and soft. He has freckles but they are so pale, the freckles, so incredibly pale that they give him a spare intermittent glow. He is very drunk most of the time, but sweetly, and he lets me wear his clothes, which I fit into because he is also soft and big and fat. He works at a garden shop in the city, a fancy one with a greenhouse, and smells of dirt and grass. During the day, I clean the flat (I learn the lingo quickly): one bedroom, a small kitchenette that opens to a small sitting area with a fire escape for a balcony. Linoleum and carpet, but clean; wood cabinets, not the cheapest; plastered walls a pale yellow, not they way they are in France, but still charming, at least charming-ish. I water his plants, which it turns out are not his plants but those of the tenant before. When I point out the irony he begins to bring home clippings. Soon they fill windowsills, shelves, fire escape, goblets of rooty green light. I sweep a lot. He has no TV, so I sit out on the fire escape a lot, too-gingerly, with the plants-and drink whatever's in the apartment and watch the traffic. One Sunday night the power goes out and some teenagers, drunk, stand down at the four corners and direct traffic all night. All night. From 8:30 p.m. or so until the sun starts to come up at 6 a.m. It lights up our corner, empty except for an early merchant or two. The baker, the bank, the grocer with flowers in front, the chip shop, the pub, the game and smoke shop. It's a lively corner with enough of everything. The light shines on the boys, first in silhouette, then in gray, then in their blue jeans and gray-blue shirts and trainers (not sneakers) and then the light catches their hair: blonde, reddish, red, brown. All of them scraggly, greasy. Boys. They look familiar and then I remember that they drink in the back of the game shop and shoot marbles or play dice and tuck cigarettes in their ears.

Danny comes home from work at 3 a.m., or from the pub after work at 3 a.m., and he gets up around noon. I make him eggs. I am pregnant. He is drunk all the time, but only on beer. I don't like beer, but I drink it, because he likes the taste. I told him my name is Mary. We will name the baby June, I think, if it's a girl, because I met Danny in June. If it's a boy, we will name him Danny, so we can call him Danny Boy.

The kettle is steaming. Danny wakes up, smelling of stale sweat and beer and he walks to the kitchen in his bare feet, reaches a hand around to my belly at the counter, then pats my behind, and takes his first smoke and tea on the fire escape. He talked wet in my ear last night, this morning, his soft wet body on me, about moving out to the country, but I like it here, where there is just enough space to see everything, and there is no screen door.

Making Space

(Honorable Mention)

By Sally Hinchcliffe

It started with the recycling. Francine's husband had mentioned it to her casually, as he left on his way to work.

"I wish you'd take it down to the paper bank," he said. "It's been piling up for weeks. Make some space in there."

It took her all morning, ferrying it down in bags on foot because taking it in the car seemed self-defeating. By the end her hands were pulled and reddened and her shoulders ached, but the space under the stairs where the newspapers had been was empty and clean. She paused to admire her work. On the breakfast table the day's paper sat, barely ruffled by her husband's brief perusal. Generally, Francine just did the crossword and glanced at the rest. Now she resented the thought of it polluting her empty space under the stairs so she took it straight down to the paper bank on her way to the supermarket and posted it in without even unfolding it. On her way back she cancelled the order with the newsagent.

The next week Francine started on the attic. Baby clothes and toys had been carefully put away and stored against a third child that had never, in the end, materialised. There was a box of blue clothes worn by her son and pink ones worn by her daughter. The lady at the Oxfam shop cooed as she unfolded them. Francine had worried that they would have become old fashioned, dated, over twenty-five years.

"Oh, look at the quality of this," the lady said. "Beautifully made." Her deft fingers folded and piled them up into stacks of pink and blue. So many clothes, thought Francine. What were we thinking?

"I've got a load more stuff at home," she said.

The wedding presents disappeared one by one, by stealth. She felt she might be making her husband anxious with her relentless clearing, but they took up so much room.

"It's hideous," Francine said, hefting a teapot in one hand. "We never use it, and we never even talk to your aunt Jo since she ran off with her driving instructor."

"It might come in handy," her husband said, and rattled the newspaper. He'd restarted their order. "And besides, it has sentimental value."

Ah yes, thought Francine, sentiment. But which one? Was it the same sentiment that had led him to keep all those letters she had found, down in the bottom of the desk drawer, even the last brief disappointed one after he had ended the affair. And since when was sentiment considered a good thing? She contemplated just dropping the teapot onto the limestone flags of the kitchen floor. They broke anything that touched them -- plates, glasses, children's heads. It would shatter and crash with a satisfying noise and then it would become rubbish, to be swept up and thrown out without any further discussion. But her husband was watching as she reached up to put it away and so her hands were steady. She had contemplated dropping the letters into the conversation in the same way, but she was saving them for later. When she really needed to clear some space. Instead, after he had gone to work, she slipped into his study and put the teapot on eBay. As she watched the bids come in she wondered how Jo was getting on with her driving instructor, and whether she had taken much with her when she ran.

"You can't throw out books," Francine's daughter said.

"I'm not throwing them out," said Francine, guiltily thinking about all those pages fluttering at her through the narrow letterbox of the paper bank, all those discarded words. They were full of other people's thoughts and she wanted to make space for her own in her head. "I'm giving them to the hospital." Her daughter helped her pack them into boxes.

"And what's this about Dad?"

"Trial separation," Francine said. Trial by fire, by jury, by ordeal, she thought. Guilty as charged, she thought. Officially it was because of the letters, the mistress, although she was long gone. But really it was about the way he came in trailing things - newspapers, CDs, little bags containing books or gadgets - and laid them down on the newly cleared surfaces of Francine's life. She remembered him at university arriving on the back of a motorbike, all his worldly possessions in a rucksack behind him, as she ferried her own belongings in, box after box, from her parents' car. Now when he left it was with a removal van, whole cubic metres of stuff gone. Francine still rang him up, for a chat, in the evenings. His voice came unchanged, uncluttered, down the line, comfortingly familiar. But when she put the phone down she looked at the empty spaces he had left with satisfaction. As her daughter loaded the books into her car, Francine called after her.

"I'm hiring a skip."

Son, daughter, husband, ferried belongings away from the skip like ants, like people caught up in a disaster, salvaging their most precious possessions. Francine looked down at them from the upstairs windows, watching dispassionately to see what they took, what they chose to leave behind. As they emptied the skip she refilled it, clearing out whole rooms. When her family had gone other scavengers arrived, picking the skip clean of saleable stuff. Francine gave them tea.

"Selling up?" one of them asked, as he paused in his rummaging and warmed his fingers on the cup she gave him.

"That's a good idea," Francine said. "Keep the mug, by the way." She put the computer itself on eBay, then closed her account. When she moved out of the house into her first flat it was in a van. When she moved into her second it was in an estate car. The first time she disappeared it was with just a backpack.

Francine found that most places she went, money stood in remarkably well for possessions. By the time she had reached India she had pared her belongings down to a bare minimum: change of clothes, toothbrush, sandals. She found a little nut-brown man who meditated under a tree in just a loincloth. For a while she sat opposite him under another tree and watched. After a while he opened his eyes and looked at her. Then he closed them again. She batted flies away and waited. With his eyes shut, he spoke.

"What are you looking for?" His accent was London inflected, she realised. His teeth full of gold.

She said, "Some space." Then, to be polite, "and what are you looking for?" He opened his eyes wide in surprise, as though nobody had ever asked him before. "Inner peace, innit," he said. "I'm here on one of those yoga retreats." That night he tried to crawl under her mosquito net while she was sleeping. "I admire you, Francine," he said. "Most women try to make space by making themselves smaller.'"

She took it as an insult and crawled out the other side, leaving him in possession of the place where she had been. She pinched the wide comfortable skin on her hips and wondered about shrinking herself, but then she laughed. That wasn't what it was all about. That wasn't it at all.

"What is it all about, Mum?" her daughter asked. She had tracked Francine down to the dusty village at the edge of the Sahara by following the breadcrumb trail of her possessions. Francine had passed into backpacker legend in the past few months, the woman who gave things away faster than she could accumulate them. "And don't say space."

Francine sighed. "I needed the space in order to think."

"Well?" said her daughter. She had grown this need for answers from somewhere.

"I thought, if I just had a little space around me, I might be able to see more clearly."

"And?" said her daughter.

"I don't know," said Francine. "I'm still looking for somewhere empty enough." They sat side by side companionably enough, but Francine sensed that her daughter had come armed with something: a plan, tickets, ultimatums. How was it that her daughter had become so bossy like this, without her, Francine, noticing? In the same way her husband had become acquisitive of things, her son someone who wiped his feet carefully before stepping on his wife's new white carpet. She felt aggrieved that people could change on her like that, without asking her permission.

"You've got to come home, Mum," her daughter said while Francine stared out at the desert's wide horizons. On the map there was just emptiness out there, a few provisional roads trailing across miles and miles of space.

"Why?" she asked. She wanted to hear something, something that would call her back, something that would drown out the siren call of the desert winds.

"Mum, I think you need some help."

That wasn't it.

The second time Francine disappeared she took nothing, not even the backpack. She walked out into the beckoning desert with just the clothes she stood up in, a scarf wrapped around her hair to shield her from the curious gazes of the men. It was early morning, the air calm without the desert wind. The sky was empty of clouds and stars, waiting for the burning sun. When she turned she could see her own footprints marring the still sand. She switched to a patch of gravel that wound through a dried up watercourse, away from the road and the houses of the village, her feet now leaving no traces. She walked in the night-chilled air of the Wadi until the sun was cresting the dunes, touching her face with warmth. Then she clambered up the shoulder of a dune where she could see the desert stretch around her and squatted down with her headscarf wrapped around her the way the locals did, only her eyes visible, and watched and waited for the day to begin.

From her vantage point, Francine could see everything. Her daughter, small, bossy, directing the search determinedly in the wrong direction. The shrugging indifference of the men being directed; the women, unaffected, going about their daily work, fetching and carrying. As the search extended past her, Francine slipped back into the village using the self-effacing walk of the women she'd watched: small steps and a careful downcast gaze rendering her invisible. She took her daughter's passport and money belt with a small mental apology to the local men who would be blamed, and scrambled up into the back of a departing pickup with four other veiled women and a dozen goats. Once in the city she swapped her headscarf for the uniform of the western tourist - water bottle, shades, sandals - and bought a ticket.

"Where to?"asked the airline woman, her eyes merely glancing off the surface of Francine's face. "London? Heathrow all right?" She clicked busily at the keyboard, not really listening to any answers. "A hundred and fifty pounds? Flying out tomorrow?" The crisp notes passed over the counter. Her daughter always was a fool with money, carried too much of it, clinging to its comforting bulk. Francine had enough for a night in a hotel and a taxi at the airport. After that there would be nothing left.

She stepped onto the plane with only the water bottle and a newspaper, one day old, still smelling of the damp of England. Mother of two missing, feared dead, it said, tucked into page nine, mentioning nowhere that the two were grown up now and bigger than she was. She stepped off with just the passport, moving lightly through the laden crowds. Once in the arrivals hall she paused to take it all in, not sure what to do next. Shops and cafes and people; trolleys canted at crazy angles, children scattering underfoot towing balloons. Her daughter's passport was buried deep in a litter bin beside Boots. She felt the sensation of having taken off a great burden, a backpack, that spine-lengthening sense of weightlessness, as though only her shoes now tethered her to the earth. Funny that it should be here, among the gray clutter of Heathrow, that she could finally find the space to think. Deep in the pit of her stomach a sensation grew and turning it, examining it from all angles, she recognised it at last, like an old friend, gone missing and returned. Loneliness. She was turning something else over now, in her hand, an angled coin, small, cool, found in the depth of her pocket. Twenty pence. A phone call. You could discard almost everything in life, but not, once memorised, numbers. As though this had been her plan all along she moved to the nearest pay phone and started dialing.

Her husband appeared to her as a collection of familiar things.

"You've still got that old jumper, then," was the first thing she said to him, to hold him off in case he was about to hug her.

"So, not dead then," he responded, leading her through the flat glaring corridors towards the car park.

"What would you have done?" Francine asked. "I came home, didn't I?" She settled into the comfortable sag of the passenger seat.

"Home?"

"Wherever that is."

"What have you done?" she asked, taking in only the way the sunlight danced over empty floors, dust motes filling the air where furniture had stood.

"I was making space," he said, touching her lightly on the elbow, nothing too proprietary, just making contact. "In case you decided to come back."

"Oh," said Francine. And then, for the first time ever, she found she had nothing left to say.

When she woke he was gone, a note beside her on the pillow. "Had to step out to work for a couple of hours. Back soon." She pulled on one of his t-shirts and her trousers, still stained and crumpled from the journey. Must buy some clothes, she thought, reflexively, and wandered into the sitting room, wanting to experience once more the shock of space he had created to call her home. He had left a couple of traces of his departure - a coffee cup, and a newspaper, barely touched, resting on the low polished space of the table. The cup was soon washed and put away, but the newspaper bothered her. Four or five times she passed and re-passed it, pacing the spaces of the flat. I'll do the crossword, she thought, picking it up and looking round for a pen. That's what I'll do, she thought, even as she was folding it up and tucking it under her arm, opening the front door, and heading out in search of a paper bank.

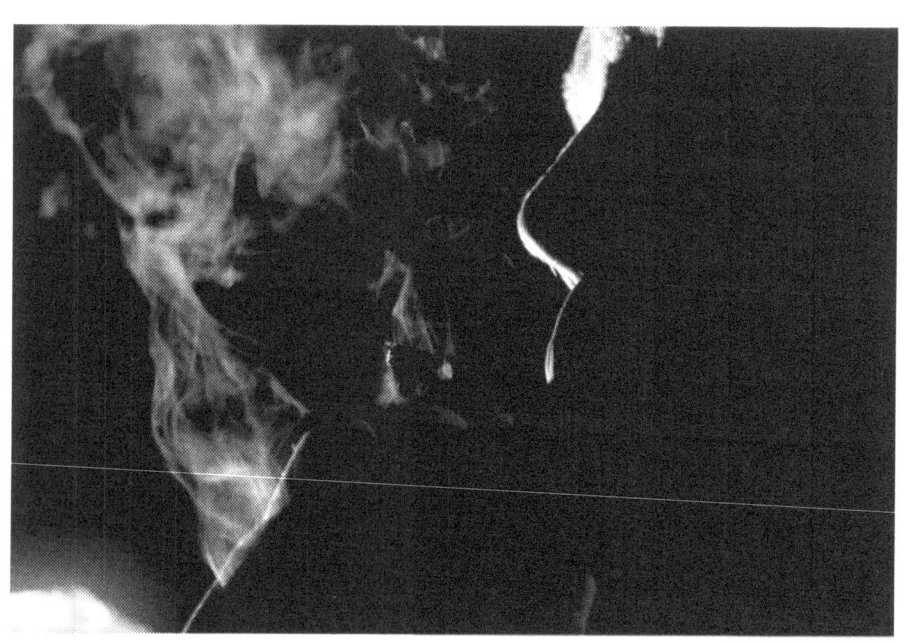

Strays

(Honorable Mention)

By Jason Jackson

Jenny took the noon bus. As they pulled out of the station, she took a last look out of the window at the city, and there, lying in the road, was a black dog. It was twitching, its guts hanging out in a red-gray mess, and as they passed, Jenny could see its eyes were a bright, sickly white.

"Strays," said the man sat across the aisle. "Always hanging around the station." He smiled at her, lines etched in his sallow skin. "Someone should do something about them."

It was as cold on the bus as it had been outside, but Jenny was tired; she smiled at the man, looked behind her at the disappearing city, and closed her eyes.

When she woke up, he was on the seat next to her. Maybe it was the cheap aftershave that had woken her. Maybe he'd coughed, said something. Maybe he had touched her. Whatever, she was awake.

"Going anywhere nice, love?" His voice was weak, and his throat rattled.

Jenny rubbed her eyes. "Edinburgh."

"Me too. Family do. Can't be bothered, to be honest, but you know what families is like."

"Wedding or something?"

"Funeral. Brother," the man sniffed. "Wanker."

The bus shuddered, swerved to the left. There was the faint sound of a horn. The man leaned closer to her momentarily, then righted himself. He smelled bad.

She sat up a little more, smoothed down her jeans. It was cold. Her neck ached from sleeping upright, and she needed a cigarette.

"Does the bus stop, do you know?" she asked, smiling a little.

"A fag you're wanting, is it?" His teeth were gray behind purple lips. "I'm the same. Can't go twenty minutes without getting the heebie-jeebies." He patted the breast pocket of his cheap suit. "Marlboro. What about you?"

"Oh, you know," she said. "Whatever's going."

"All you young girls smoke, nowadays." His breath smelt old, rotten. "Still. We can share, if you want. When we stop."

She turned to her reflection in the window. She was a ghost, the bare trees and grey fields sweeping through her.

"I'm Harold. Harry," he said.

"Jenny," she said, not turning.

"Pleased to meet you, and all that."

"Yeah."

Outside, it started to rain, although there didn't seem to be any clouds, just an unbroken grey-whiteness. Drops began to run almost horizontally across the pane as the bus hurtled along. Jenny felt her eyes closing again, and she brought her feet up from the floor.

Next to her, she could hear Harry breathing quietly.

When she woke the bus was pulling into a service station. It was still cold, but the rain had stopped.

"About bloody time," said Harry.

People all around them were standing, stretching. He shifted in his seat. "You coming for a fag?"

She tried to stand, hunched over. "Yeah."

"Your wish is my command," said Harry. He patted another pocket and smiled. "Bet you could do with a drink as well."

She smiled, looked away. They waited as the rest of the passengers shuffled down the aisle, then followed.

At the plastic table, Harry topped up his coffee from his hip-flask.

"Whiskey?" said Jenny.

"Warms you up, it does."

"I've never had whiskey in coffee before"

He looked at her, smiled, and poured. When Jenny lifted the mug to her lips the coffee spilled a little over the edges.

"Don't waste it," he said.

She blew on the surface, sipped. "It's nice."

"Can't beat it."

There were lots of people all around them. Some kids were playing in a plastic play area full of coloured balls. There was a smell of chips, burgers, vomit.

"Thanks for the fag," she said. "And the drink."

"Got to look after each other, haven't we? People like us."

Jenny sipped her coffee. "People like us?"

"I saw you at the station," said Harry. "Young girl like you, all alone. No one to see you off." He sipped his drink, smiled. "People like us, we stick together."

"I'm meeting my dad in Edinburgh."

"That's nice," said Harry. His eyes were washed-out. "How old are you, love?"

She clenched her fist under the table, took a drag from her cigarette. "Eighteen."

He was looking at her now, staring right into her eyes. He said, "I remember being young. Didn't have a fucking clue." There was no smile. His mouth was a line across his face. "Headstrong. I ran away from home as well." He sipped his coffee, reached for the flask, and topped-up his mug. "Not a bloody clue."

"I'm not on my own," said Jenny, fists hard. "I'm not running away. I'm meeting my dad."

"Yeah. You said, love." He put his fags back in his pocket.

Under the table, she felt his shoe touch hers, then quickly pull away.

Back on the bus, she walked up the aisle behind him. They were late, the engine already running. All the seats were full, apart from their own.

"Sit next to the window, if you want," she said.

Harry shook his head. "Makes me sick. Can't stand seeing the world rushing past so quick."

Jenny squeezed past him, and sat down. The bus inched out of the car-park.

"How long to Edinburgh?' she said."

"Bloody hours, love." He settled into his seat, coughing. "You want to play a game?"

She smiled thinly. "Not really."

"I got cards."

"I think I'll sleep."

"Suit yourself, love," said Harry, looking at her.

It was dark when she woke again, and Harry was asleep next to her, snoring quietly. His mouth hung open, and a line of saliva glistened on his chin as car headlights streaked through the window. His face was grey, older. Jenny turned away from him. Outside was darkness, she could see her reflection, and behind her, Harry. Every time a car passed going the other way, the image of the two of them disappeared in the flash of light. Jenny watched herself disappear and reappear, with Harry behind her, all the way until they reached the outskirts of the city.

"Looks like he's forgotten about you," said Harry. They were waiting to get their bags from under the bus, behind a scrum of passengers. It was freezing.

"He's just late."

"Not good, a young girl like you, out here on your own." Harry sniffed as he looked around the bus station. "Some funny people around."

"He'll be here soon." She could see her bag, but there were too many bodies in the way.

"Want me to wait with you?"

"I'm fine, thanks." She made a lunge through a gap and grabbed the handle of her rucksack.

"That all you got, girl?" he said.

"I can't carry much." She shrugged one strap over her shoulder.

"You need someone to look after you, that's what you need."

The crown of passengers was thinning out, and as Harry reached down to get his suitcase, Jenny walked away. There were taxis, people, buses. It was late, but still busy. She stood at the curb, hesitating.

"You want a fag for the wait?" He was behind her.

She turned. "Thanks." She took one from the packet, hand shaking from the cold.

He took a cigarette for himself, and began to play with the packet, flipping it over and over in his palm. "Listen, I know what I must seem like. You hear all these stories. Pedos, and all that." He coughed as he looked around him, and his skin was yellow in the old light of the station. "I'm staying at my brother's place, with his wife, just 'til the funeral, like." Finally, he looked at her, and laughed. "She can't stand me, to be honest. But I'm family. It's expected."

She took his lighter, clicked the flame. "My dad'll be here in a minute."

He put his case down, shrugged his shoulders. "All I'm saying is, you might need a friend." He got a pen from inside his jacket, and wrote on the fag packet. "I'll give you her number, just in case, like." He held it out to her. "She might be a hard-faced bitch, but just between you and me, she's all right, is Gabby."

Jenny looked at the packet in his hand. The top was open, and there were still a few cigarettes inside.

"I'll be there for a couple of nights. Then I'm off back home again." He shook the packet so it rattled. "Take them."

She smiled at him quickly, grabbed the packet, and stuffed it into her pocket. "Thanks."

"Listen, if your dad doesn't turn up, or you get home sick, or anything, phone me at Gabby's. I'll stand you the ticket for the return journey." He picked up his case with one hand, and reached out with the other. Before Jenny could pull away, he touched her cheek with his thumb and fingertips. "Just a kid," he said.

A taxi pulled up to the rank at the exit of the station. There was a screech of brakes and a yelp. A dog ran up onto the pavement, limping madly from where it had glanced off the taxi, and Jenny saw its eyes flash as it ran passed her.

"You get them in every city," said Harry. He didn't look at her as he turned away. "I'll see you, love," he said.

Jenny watched him walk towards the taxi rank. He was moving slowly, leaning with the weight of his case. She touched her pocket, feeling for the packet of cigarettes, and looked back to the road. The dog was gone.

At last, there was a gap in the traffic, and Jenny disappeared into it.

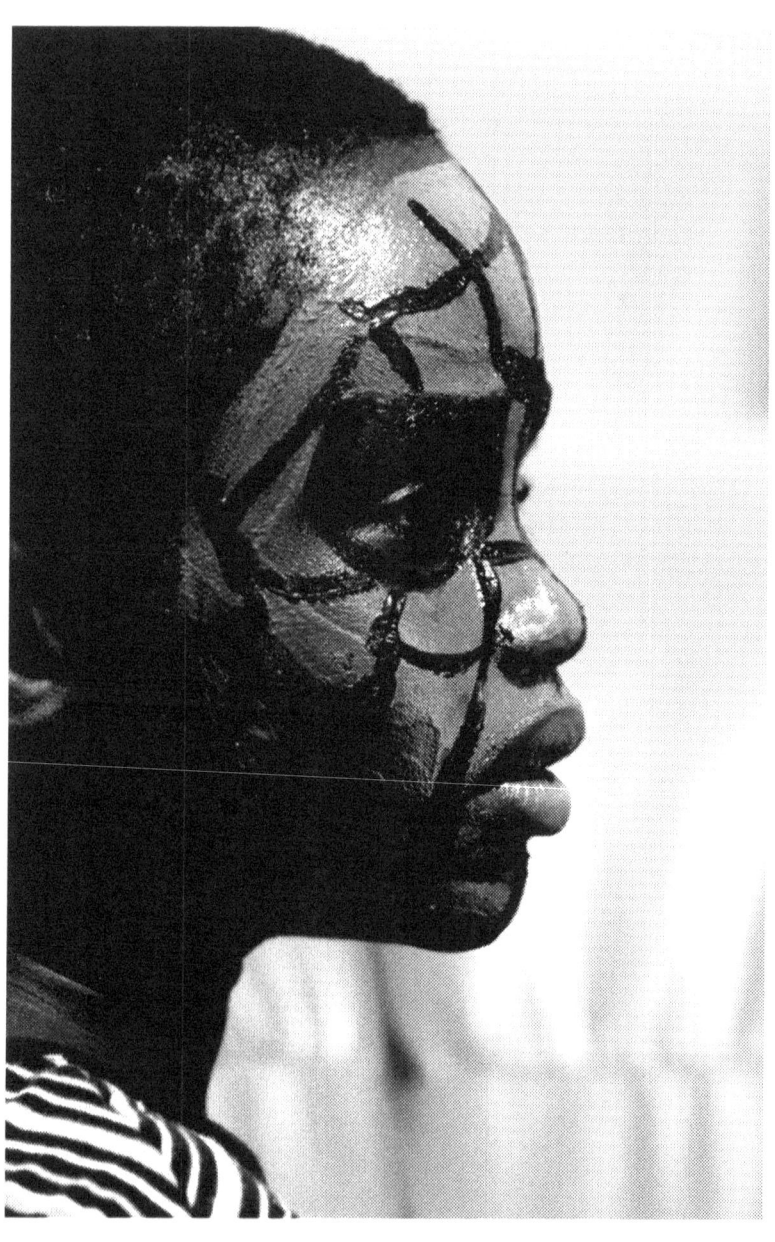

Pleasing Mother

By Leonard Kenyon

Milton Harner despised his name.

"Milton ... Milton ... MILTON!!!"

"Coming, mother."

And it had always been this way.

John Harner had abandoned his family leaving his son to fend for himself at just six weeks old, and although Milton knew nothing of the man other than what little mother had been loathe to share, he'd come to suspect that his father had simply left because he'd begun to detest the sound of his own name as well. And for that, Milton had never blamed him.

"Milton, for god sakes, don't touch that. Milton, put that down you could hurt yourself. Milto,n don't track mud all over the house. Milton, wash up. Milton, that's not for touching. Milton, that's not for sitting. Milton, put a coat on you'll catch a cold. Milton, my tea is too hot. Milton, it's my medication time. Milton. Milton. MILTON."

Milton never made very many friends in school, certainly none that mother approved of. Milton didn't go to college because mother became ill. Milton never had a job because mother forbid it, and so Milton never moved out of his mother's beige colonial on Rose Terrace. Milton was forty-three years old.

"What is it, mother?"

"I want to go to the drug store."

"For what, mother?"

"Why do you think, you simpleton? Get our coats."

"Yes, mother."

* * *

Mother drove while Milton sat glum, soberly considering the wheel and slamming the car into on-coming traffic, killing them both. And although mother scrutinized almost every aspect, every nook and cranny of her son's life, she did not know this: Milton was losing his mind.

"If that girl is working the counter today and I have to wait in line, Jim is going to get a big piece of my mind," mother promised and then turned their beast of a Buick onto another street. Milton nodded and mumbled agreement, both essential for survival in her company, but really, really he was thinking only of doors: One kept locked in the basement of mother's house and one kept locked in the basement of his mind.

She went on oblivious of the insanity sitting next to her or the death that was welcomed in his heart. "Just the other day Sadie Raferdy told me that she waited in line for twenty-two minutes and there was hardly anyone in the store, and it was because that girl was on the telephone."

A door in the house, a door in his head.

"Milton! You're slouching, sit up straight."

"Yes, mother."

When the second door opens, Mother will be . . .

* * *

Milton helped her out of their brown boat onto the sidewalk and offered to go in himself, not that he wanted to; beyond the driveway of mother's house he was often overwhelmed with anxiety and even terror, and though their trips into town were seldom, he hated them more and more each time. Maybe it was the infrequency at fault for making him feel as though every outing was a brand new introduction into the contempt of the public eye, or maybe it was just mother: Mother's nit picking, Mother making a scene, Mother embarrassing him and the people around her, turning them green - but if he didn't at least offer, he would certainly hear about it later. But mother only grunted past him, and as he watched her lumber her way through the first set of mechanical doors into the foyer, one of those basement doors, his basement door finally opened the slightest crack.

"Mother?" he spoke after her.

She turned, almost knocking over a rack of pamphlets and then barked, "What, Milton, What?"

"Do you know how long you'll be? I was going to go to the store," He said and pointed across the lot in an elbow the buildings made to the supermarket.

"No." She said with finality and began to turn away.

"Mother?"

"What, Milton, God damn it. What?"

"Would you like anything?"

"Oh, for Christ sakes, here."

She unclasped her purse and handed him a ten, "Get me a raspberry tea and a bag of circus peanuts. You can keep the change, but boy, don't you dare get any candy or sweets yourself, your complexion is bad enough."

His complexion had been nothing but perfect for nearly twenty years but he kept his mouth shut, besides he didn't want to argue; he wanted to smile. When she was out of sight, he hurried down the walk and entered the hardware store, without so much as giving the supermarket a second look.

* * *

The weed killer was heavy in his hands but the weight of its irreversible possibilities excited him; it was the key, it was the shoehorn, it was the battering ram. Of course, there would be no going back once it was done - but he had come this far, he had his hand on the latch and once he lifted it all the way and let that sliver of light on the other side of that door, his door, finally engulf him -- he'd be okay, and no one would ever know -- everything would be . . .

"Can I help you sir?"

That door slammed tightly closed.

Milton heard a nervous and befuddled, "no thanks you" escape his throat before he nearly dropped the jug onto the floor and then scurried back down the isle empty handed.

It was no good. This is no good; that man knew, he thought frantically, and he knows what you've been planning Milty, and it won't be much longer now before he tells the authorities -

He needed out.

At the midway crossroads of Home and Outdoor Furnishings, his eyes feverish on the door, another door, one with a rubber runner pad and a neon orange exit sign above it and a metal railing to its right and left for the occasional unpredictable cart pusher, one that wouldn't scare or slam shut leaving its eager passer destitute and hopeless - a woman with a cart full of soil sideswiped him.

Milton fell back into a shelf lined with screws and washers, his glasses going crooked on his beak of a nose and then the woman gasped. At first he thought, oh god she knows too, she knows what I planned to do, but when she finally spoke, he wished he'd been right.

"Milton? Milton Harner, is that you?"

He stopped jockeying with his glasses and stared blankly.

"It's me, Margaret Bowen, well, Mary Barringer now," she held up her hand showing the ring, "How have you been?"

Milton began to shuffle in place looking for a way around her, but she seemed not to notice, "I live in Washington now. I'm home for a few weeks; mom is selling the house and I'm helping her with the yard," she said and pointed to the soil in her cart, "What about you?"

Milton's knees were growing rubbery and his head dizzy. He couldn't speak, he would need to leave soon or Mary would be picking him up off of the floor. And Mary or Margaret, or whatever she was going by these days, hadn't needed to reintroduce herself; he'd been jerking off to her memory for decades - his luck was bullshit. This thought painted his cheeks and brow in the color of roses.

Milton scurried away back down the isle he'd come towards the gardening section again without a word, leaving Mary Barringer to stand as dumbfounded in the intersection as the man in the green apron had in the gardening section moments before.

* * *

It was now or never. He veered far along the backside of the store with his head down and brought the weed killer to the checkout. There was only one register going and a herky-jerky man held up the front, shouting something about a miss-marked price of a hammer, but Milton couldn't hear the words. He paced from heal to heal, How long had he already been gone? Sweat beaded at his temples and forehead and ran into his eyes -- if he didn't get the weed killer in the trunk of mother's car before her prescriptions were filled, his door would stay shut forever. Oh god the jug seemed to weigh a thousand pounds, and every available eye was fixed and glaring on him -- they knew; they all knew.

Milton paid with mother's ten and ran out the door crossing the parking lot and making a B-line for the Buick. He was nearly struck by a red car as it backed out a little too fast and a little too wildly from a space next to a cart corral, but he barely noticed; time was short, even if the phone talking girl mother hated so was working the prescription counter, time was short.

If mother was already waiting for him or happened out the door, or if the law came racing after him, he would drop the jug and pray they didn't see and if they did, deny it until he turned blue, but when he reached the car, it was alone and to find it empty.

He popped the trunk and raced around to the back, sweat running in streams now, and just as he was setting the jug deep behind the spare tire, mother came huffing back out of the drugstore with her prescription bag clutched in one meaty hand, bouncing and jostling at her hip.

"What are you doing? Get away from there. It's filthy back there, you'll ruin your clothes," she bellowed.

"I was just checking the spare, mother."

"Why? You're no mechanic. Now get out of there."

"Yes, mother."

He shut the trunk and helped her around to the driver's side, trying to stifle the smile that wanted to give the secret away.

"Where's my tea?" she asked, settling into her seat.

"What?" he said.

"My tea! Are you daft boy?"

He froze hearing the hinges of his door creaking shut again and it at least wiped even the thought of that Judas smile clean from his face. He closed her door and went around to his side passing the trunk and having to resist the insane urge to check and make sure the green key was still there, still real. But what was he going to tell her, what was he going to say? Lies had never fallen free from his tongue; mother always knew; mother was all seeing, her eyes the yellowing, beaded equivalent of the breaking hours in an interrogation room. What he wanted to say was, "Yes mother I am daft. You see, I planned on killing you tonight but I fucked that up so now maybe I'll just hang myself in the closet tonight after your bath instead." But instead, he climbed into the passenger side and said nothing.

"Well?" she asked, waiting to put the car into gear.

"Don't be mad, mother,

But I

"But I

Bought some poison to kill you with

"Bought, donated, the money to the church." He spoke serenely, not knowing if it had sounded phoney or if his voice had wavered in pace with his heart. There was a seemingly infinite pause, and then mother snorted at his stupidity.

"That's the last time I give you money for anything; you sap. You know that money just goes to buy the minister a new car, or to keep his Jezebel quiet."

He sighed, hoping it would sound like a breath of shame rather than relief, and knowing that he'd just been very lucky.

Mother put the car in gear and began backing out without so much as a second glance at him and that was good, because though the lie he'd just told had come out convincingly and calmly, his door had been slamming over and over and over.

Mother didn't want to go straight home. Mother wanted to stop at the cleaners and a tag sale to look at a gaudy sugar bowl. But Milton didn't mind and sat in the car smiling for the first time in years as Mother did what Mother did.

* * *

Days passed but still no opportunity arose and so Milton's purchase stayed hidden in the depths of mother's trunk, but it was not forgotten. Every night after dinner and her bath and then when after she'd finally retired to her room down the hall, he sat quietly in his bedroom's window peering down on the Buick. And after the third day of doing so, he no longer tried to sleep; the trunk beat in the center of his thoughts like the Tell Tale Heart and he quickly found that even in the daylight there was no rest from it.

Milton also began to realize that his opportunity may never come and that unless he made a move, it might actually slip away for good - And then the medication times and baths and game shows and embarrassments and fear and hatred and control would continue on until they had even outlived the very house he was indentured by guilt and despair to. And he would need to hurry, because with every passing and rising sun, the anger and humiliation that had driven him down the isles of the hardware store were slowly fading into the lonely hopelessness that had kept him right where he was for so long, and with it, his door inched ever shut.

And so there he sat, peering and waiting and slipping deeper and deeper. Even the other door, the real door, the one in the basement of the real house in the real world, had for the first time begun to seem pointless and dull, and the long kept secret behind its wood and hinge held no precedent over the thump of the green heart in the trunk.

But then . . .

Dinner was eaten in front of their television; it was safe to say that Pat and Alex were the only dinner guests the Harner's had ever entertained. Milton got mother's medication ready and helped her into her recliner - "The water was too warm to take pills with. The television wasn't loud enough. And he was surely taking his sweet time, her shows were almost on, awful moron." And while mother settled into her nightly routine of ingesting a thousand pills and conspirializing the last quarter of the evening news, Milton slipped into the basement…

He'd never been so daring, especially with her in the house, and it threatened to make him sick. But he'd decided that it was time, as the jug beat and danced and hollered and moaned in the night, and he wanted to see the other side of that door, the old door, the real door, before his opened forever.

He cringed as the stairs creaked beneath him and as an outburst of mother's deranged brand of laughter came stabbing through the floorboards above him, but when he reached the bottom landing, his heart slowed a bit as the distance between himself and her grew.

He crept to the far end to the door, the real door, and moved his hands above along its frame in the foundation for the tiny key ring. Behind tumble, chain, and hinge was kept a few of John's long abandoned and forgotten belongings, among them a record player and a handful of warping and disincarnating albums, but one still worked, and it was the only one Milton ever had played anyway - and when on those nights in the late hours after mother had gone to sleep to begin dreaming the dreams of a thousand petulant and wicked hags, and only on the bluest of blue moons when he was at his most daring, he played it over and over until the image of mother's eyes beating on his back full of fearfulness and scorn, became too much. And though the room where he loved but feared to go was a far dark place in place that mother had long since gone for her fear of the old cellar stairs and mice and spiders, and a place that even seemed to have been forgotten by her entirely - the peace the music brought was only ever fleeting - but the green heart and the other door, his door- that would be forever.

He must have put the keys in his room again; he sometimes would accidentally bring it back with him; befuddled and anxious, not being able to flee the basement fast enough, and then on his next venture, at times years passing between them, he would have to turn right back around and that usually meant the end of it. But tonight he'd wanted to hear those sweet melodies if not for one last time, for the road so to speak. Tonight he'd wanted to place the headphones on again and set the needle down and then sit on his father's suitcase. He'd wanted to trace the two-toned orange block letters on the album's cover, letters which shouted a single word he could wholeheartedly relate to, and as he'd done all the times before.

He often wondered what mother thought of the group he'd come to love so, that had become the pivot point in his teetering sanity, but figured she would dismiss and hate them on principle; the album had once belonged to John of course but Milton also guessed she'd be of the mind who had seen the group at the time and probably still did, as being the very route cause for suggesting if not blatantly introducing fornication and drugs to the then previously innocent and impressionable minds of the wholesome American youth. But it wasn't so much as the worry over what mother would think that had made this door such a guarded and desired thing, but rather and simply it was about what she didn't know.

He'd found it when he was ten, never knowing before that a piece of his father lay just below him. There had been an accident outside on the street and it had marked the only time he'd openly defied her wishes, consequently sending mother to the hospital with palpitations, and in all the commotion he'd been left behind, momentarily granted a window in her umbilical and omnipotent supervision. And as mother sat in the ER downtown clutching her chest and cursing the doctor for not seeing that she knew more about the medical field than he, he'd wondered downstairs and found the door and the keys. But on this night the key was probably in his bottom drawer hidden in a sock, and they were no help to him now.

Milton crept back up the basement stairs and poked his head from the cellar door. The back of mother's sparsely curled head could be seen through the kitchen and living room archway as she sat impatiently anticipating that first spin of the wheel. In any moment now, she would be expecting her dinner because that was the way it had always been.

While their dinners were microwaving, Milton went out to the car as quietly as he'd gone to the basement and gently opened the trunk. It was still there, though the jug seemed disappointingly dull in the unlit driveway; seen it no longer beat or danced; it just was.

He brought it silently in through the side door and set it on the kitchen counter. Mother cackled at the television from the other room, almost causing him to knock it to the floor, but he held on and unscrewed the top, wincing at the rough plastic snap of it and then shuddered a second time as Mother let loose another thick chortle from her chair.

Then, Milton brought their steaming dinners in and set them on their respective T.V trays.

He sat waiting and watching as impatient as mother, but neither for Pat nor his wheel, but rather the first bite of mother's last meal.

"Milton, I need another glass of water," she said and then scoffed at a pretty girl on the television.

"Yes, mother."

When Milton returned from the kitchen with mother's drink, she was eating. Oh yes she was, she was eating.

Gobble it up you bitch, he thought wildly, gobble it down like a good bitch.

He sat and watched her, intently eating his own meal, as she went on shovelling it in and scolding the game show contestants for making poor choices and not solving the puzzle as always. And as always, guessing blindly and doing a laughable job herself.

But that will all be over soon old Milty, he thought and had to shovel food into his own face to keep himself from laughing madly.

But the anticipation was going to kill him. His stomach turned in knots. Sweat ran down his neck and he wiped it away with a careful eye on her. Then, during a commercial for Zoltreck (a mood enhancer with a thousand possible side effects, ask your doctor if it's right for you), mother choked and slumped in her chair.

Milton stared at her.

She did not move.

The door was open.

Mother was dead.

Milton continued staring, working the last bite of his own TV dinner down. But the immediate relief he'd expected hadn't come but rather disappointment like the jug in the low light. And the relief wasn't going to come was it? Had he actually believed this would make him happy? Because now that it was done, he wished it were him sitting there. He was a terrible person. He was a terrible son. What would life be now without her? Mother was all he knew. He hadn't thought it threw. And looking at her now - little bits gravy clinging in the crow cracks around her mouth and the whiskers on her chin, slumped down in her chair like an old, fat, rag doll - was making him feel awfully sick to his stomach.

Milton began to hyperventilate. He began to cry. He would have to turn himself in and except the consequences; there was no other way.

He stood to go to the phone, set on repentance and amendments, and staggered knocking over his TV tray. He then watched horrified and guilty as the cardboard carton tumbled across the floor, leaving a dollop trail of runny gravy like boot prints in the snow, soiling and ruining mother's perfect carpet. He looked at his mother sheepishly and then down at the stains but strangely they began to fade and change like a flower on one of those "hippy" cartoons mother had always forbid - His vision was blurry. And come to think of it now, his head pounded.

Milton took another step towards the phone and stumbled onto the floor joining the mess he'd made, and then began vomiting foamy clots all over himself. His muscles tensed and locked. He could go no further.

Mildred Harner opened her eyes and watched as her dim witted son wriggled and writhed in misery on her ruined carpet. She wondered if the idiot knew now what she always had: A mother's love can be dangerous sure, but a mother's mistrust can be deadly.

Oh, how she'd always known he'd try something like this, and oh how she'd always been right; like father like son.

As Milton lay dying on the floor he thought he could hear the tinkle of keys and his mother's voice singing a familiar tune. And it had never sounded more unlovely, "Help me if you can, I'm feeling down . . ."

Just the One

(Honorable Mention)

By Jordan Kushins

Cookie had been working at The Mermaid for as long as I'd been going there. She was ancient, an amazing Technicolor relic preserved in Aqua-Net and Max Factor, voice like an unholy union of cigarettes and strawberry milkshakes and that nametag with a little sticker of a chocolate chip dotting the "i" always pinned lopsided on that luscious old rack of hers. Don't know why she even bothered with it; most everybody coming into the 'Maid had been in there a hundred times or more.

She could have been someone, maybe, but she whiled away the years making old men happy and young men wonder, satisfied somehow with the copper coin tips left in the coffee mug rings on the once sparkly Formica tables. Every time I pushed through that door, the little bell would tinkle lightly. Every time it was the same familiar game.

"Hi there, Sweetie. Just the one today?" she'd ask. Always just the one; I was a solitary sonofabitch, and the diner, though never full, was full of my kind: loners and losers looking for a place to call home. I'd give her a nod and a wink, she'd raise her eyebrows and smirk; she knew my type. She had to, we filled up every other seat. She would grab a menu from the counter with a sly '...right this way...' and weave between the tables and chairs, sneakers across the black and white checkered parquet, an intricate dance performed easy as apple pie. I'd follow her, close enough to catch a whiff of her rose-scented perfume through the heavy smell of stale coffee and onion rings that lingered over the one-room joint like a greasy haze.

It was a hot summer, even for Arizona. I spent my time at The Mermaid in the booth by the window, minutes into hours into days and weeks and months, all on the price of a root beer float or two, a few burgers, and a couple of side orders of fries. And the temperature just kept rising. Monday was solid but Tuesday the world was melting. A fan on the countertop oscillated air as thick as mayonnaise through the tiny space. Cookie was sitting on a stool- plumb stuck for all I knew- fanning herself with a menu. She didn't even bother getting up when I walked in. I knew the routine, though, could do the dance myself by now. I made it over to the booth and slid in.

"How about a little something to cool you off, Hot Stuff?" Her voice across the restaurant. The voice.

"Vanilla coke, please, Cookie," I said. "Nice and cold. Something to go down easy, real smooth."

"Something sweet for a Sweet Thing. Coming right up, hun," she said. The backs of my legs were sweating, pale skin against faded denim against the electric blue vinyl of the banquette that was peeling away from the corners and had a chunk of stuffing missing from a hole that I picked at sometimes. But it felt good to sit down. I didn't mind so much about sticking: not in my booth, not in the Mermaid.

She took her time with the drink, didn't rush filling the glass up or making her way over to the table. She might have moved slower but the spark was still there, fanned by the flames of the heat wave. I watched her, the curves of her body shifting beneath the candy-striped dress stretched across her hips. She was sweating too: through her clothes, on her chest and her face, dark roots at the hairline even darker with perspiration, beads at her temples dissolving into trickles down her cheeks. There was nothing to do but keep on sweating. The familiar two-step, a classic waltz, she ambled over and placed the glass of soda on the laminate surface. Three maraschino cherries bobbed on top between the crushed ice. She leaned on her hip, fleshy thigh pushing up against the chrome edging of the Formica, pink cotton bulging with the heft of her thick leg. I couldn't help but look and it was too hot to pretend I didn't care. My eyes caught the swelled form just long enough. Eye contact. She noticed all right.

"What'll it be then, Sugar? You ready for something to eat?" she asked.

"Always ready," I said.

"I figured as much."

"You know me too well."

"Indeed. What'll it be then?"

"I'll have a burger please, Cookie."

"Medium-well, extra pickles, special sauce on the side and hold the mayo?"

"There you go again."

"I'm not going anywhere."

"Thank god for that."

It went like that. I willed her to sit down with me. I thought if I looked at her right, nipped her eye just so, she might forget that she was working; she might overlook that I was nothing but an old chump. I held out hope that for a moment she would forget, and I might be someone more exciting or enticing than no one special pushing the wrong side of a half-dollar. She didn't sit down though, not today. Not ever. I couldn't manage the trick. Instead she turned, heavy sashay to the counter. She wasn't going fast, at least, or far.

I speared a cherry with the straw and popped it in my mouth, pulled the stem out from between my teeth and placed it on the damp napkin. The polished chrome of the jukebox caught the sun and the glint caught my eye; it was unrelenting, the brightness of the glare and the heat. I had to squint even indoors. I glimpsed my reflection in the metal napkin holder, all distorted, like a mirage or a crazy fun house mirror. My nose was too big for my face, but I knew that without looking. I rubbed the prominent bumpy ridge down the middle, broken only the once. But once was enough; one time to leave me with a mug to remember.

It wasn't all bad, though, to look broken. I could be comfortable at The Mermaid, a local place for local people all battered and tattered and beat to shit or tired of making out like they could belong anywhere else but a busted old dive like this. If I were polished and glossy I wouldn't belong. Or I'd belong somewhere else, that's for damn sure. But here I was, and my luck wasn't changing any quicker than I was getting smoother as the hands on the neon clock on the wall clicked around and around.

It had been a long time. Cookie had the banter, but I never once felt her skin, or her dress, rested my cheek over the small birthmark on her collarbone, ran my hands through her hair or stroked my fingers down her neck, and down, and down. I thought about it. Thought about doing all those things and more, right there on the booth where I sat by myself and played with a dirty spoon or the ketchup bottle or picked at that hole in the seat, imagining other things. Sometimes I could only think about Cookie; what she smelled like up real close and whether she tasted of beer batter or French's mustard after a long double shift.

Sometimes, though, only the real stuff bounced back and forth through my head, pinballing around, stuff I had lived and breathed and knew, stuff that validated that I had a past, that I had existed once beyond these walls. Stuff like palling around with Flo. Oh man oh man oh man, she used to kiss me, and kiss me good. When she did I thought no one's face could ever get that close to mine. I thought about how I kept my eyes closed, and how I opened them sometimes just to check and her eyelids, all caked and creased shadow and crooked liner, her eyelids told me that she loved me. They rested shut, all easy, like they never had to open again; like they finally didn't have to look anymore. Florence, with her brash Brooklyn accent like a siren's wail in small town Mesa, with her green leather handbag with the snapped strap held together by a safety pin. She called me 'rugged' when she sat on my lap and bit my bottom lip, just hard enough, 'tough' when she asked and asked and asked and I never had any answers. She let me take her in the backseat of her powder blue Coupe-de-Ville the first night we met. A smooth ride, that was. I could have girls like Flo. I could be with women who were broken too. God, it really had been a while. A cloudy patch drifted in out of nowhere, fleeting, merciful shade from the pounding sun. I wiped my brow with the back of my hand, wiped the back of my hand on my jeans. Cookie was perched on her stool again, doing the daily crossword. Her horn-rimmed glasses roosted on her own prominent bumpy ridge, and she called out the downs and acrosses through the hatch to the overweight chef.

"Alright Sammy, gimme a nine-letter word for "One who watches". Second letter might be "p", fourth is definitely a "c"," she said.

Sam carried on flipping yolks and patties, his body's dull mechanics swaddled in heaps and heaps of pasty flesh, wrapped then again in stained t-shirt and food-splattered apron. He was a fixture, like Cookie, a living, breathing, bona-fide part of the scene, a sweaty mass regardless of the season, a marvel with a grill and a deep fryer. Cookie tapped her pencil on the ashtray and bits of ash jumped out to freedom onto the newsprint, until she swept them away with her hand onto the floor.

I was the spectator. I turned to stare out the window. People were walking by, carrying on with lives I would never have anything to do with. They passed by each other like nothing at all. I liked to think that watching the world kept me involved, that it was better somehow than completely shutting down. I was more at ease observing than participating, better at judging than being judged. But I knew it. I was aware that it was the easy way out, I wasn't trying to fool anyone. I looked hard but lived soft. It was safe for me here on the other side of the glass.

A plate was placed on the table in front of me, juicy burger and a few sneaky fries.

"Medium-well, extra pickles, special sauce on the side and hold the mayo. And I'll get you another vanilla Coke," Cookie said.

"You're too good to me."

"Only the best for the best."

Cookie. Yeah, she could have done something. She could have made a real living, anything other than serving poor saps like me. She deserved better, and I'm sure we deserved worse, but we all got by together. Afloat but adrift, we got by, dropping anchor when we could in and out of the Mermaid. I put my hands to the bun and squeezed. A greasy trail ran down my pinky finger, down the side of my hand and my wrist and my arm and I took in a mouthful. She slid through the tables, picking up a few empty coffee mugs and dirty plates. Humming. Beyond the sea, she and Bobby Darin, then the slow twirl, then the fleshy strut back to her counter, to her puzzle, to her life across the diner from mine.

"Sam, five-letter word for "Benevolence"," she said. The pencil eraser rested between her lips and she stared down at the paper.

"You and those puzzles, Cooks," he answered. "If you're asking me, you're asking the wrong guy. I haven't got the foggiest, never have, never will. Words, you know... they, uh... they ain't really my thing."

Cookie put down her pencil. She stared at me. I ran my fingers over my mouth, checking for wayward crumbs. She stared past me and out the window. Her fingers ran along the hem of her collar, always like that, always when she got the gaze. Maybe she thought about when life was different. Maybe it never was. But she had that look in her eye, that distance. She was stuck there for so long, too long, but had the window as escape and she could leave whenever she wanted, just like I had the dirty spoon and the ketchup and Flo. One of the old timers, a real prize crank, broke the spell.

"Hey, Cookie, it wouldn't hurt to take an order around here every once in awhile. I'll have another cream soda." He spat when he talked, and wore the same brown trousers every goddamn day. Cookie called him Sweetie and Kid and Bub as well. We were all the same to her.

She made the journey back to the diner like nothing, big smile and even a wink for the ungrateful git as she slipped out of her seat and poured another pop. My food had disappeared and my fingertips were slick and there was a dollop of ketchup on the table and a small piece of pickle in my lap. I took a few napkins and cleaned myself up, careful to wipe my chin and sweep off any crumbs into my palm, then sprinkle them back on the plate. On her way back to the counter she stopped at my table.

"Looks like you're doing alright over here," she said.

"Never better," I replied.

"Can I get you anything else?"

"I'm doing just fine with what I've got. Thanks though, Cookie."

"Just doing my job, Pet."

The truth. She was just doing her job. The turn, the shuffle...

"Oh, Cookie..." I said. Any excuse.

"Yeah, hun?"

""Mercy"."

"Huh?"

""Mercy"." Five-letter word for "Benevolence"."

And she smiled that smile, that smile that would keep me going to the end of my days, come rain or shine or sleet or hail. That twinkle would get me through.

"Well, whaddya know," she said. "Always full of surprises, this place. And it's not even noon yet." It was her turn to wink.

"It's never too early for the unexpected to happen," I said.

"Or too late, Love."

"Well we'd better be ready, then," I said.

"You betcha. Say, what would I do without you here at the 'Maid?'" Marry rich, write a book, hit the streets, win the lottery, go broke at the track, save the whales, move to California, stay in Mesa, have a burger, skip the fries, make a friend, make amends, be discovered, lose your lunch, bite your nails, shed some pounds, miss me dearly, move on quickly...

"I dunno, Cookie. But I promise to come back tomorrow just so you don't have to find out."

And off she went. The air was still and I was sweating through my shirt. I took a napkin and wiped my brow, then put it down on the table and picked up the bottle of Heinz.

One Afternoon

By Joleen Kuyper

Puddles, cigarette butts everywhere, crisp bags and sweet wrappers, good old-fashioned dirt. A sea of rubbish and ashes. The walls adorned with badly spelled words, bad grammar, better than some of the meanings though; Jen luvs Jez, Sammy woz ere. Cum on u reds. IRA RooL. Sonia a whore for sure. Mickey shags sheeps.

This is their place. These are their names, their teams, their feelings, their political affiliations. Their cigarette butts. I wish I smoked. I wish I was a bad girl, then they might just leave me alone. I don't even merit a line on the wall, a badly-spelled bad word. All the same, I know I exist to them.

Why am I here, their place? What if they were to find me here - there's only one way out - what then? They won't find me here, because they are looking for me, they would never think to look here, in their lair. I am smarter than them; I hope.

I am hiding from them. Other people tell me they are hiding too. Magazines, my mother, my older brother. Hiding from themselves, they say. I am hiding from them too; we have so much in common.

I am wet and cold, crouching in this puddle, this lake with floating debris, sweet wrappers and cigarette butts, greasy red lipstick still around the ones the girls smoked. The water doesn't wash it away. Maybe I'll catch a cold, then I'll be able to stay at home tomorrow, stay in bed. Escape it for another day, just procrastination.

I need to go to the toilet, I can't leave here till it gets dark, they are looking for me, they might find me, I must hold it in, I must distract myself, if I leave here they will see me, the more I try to be invisible in a crowd the more I stand out.

I have my books with me, I can't take them out, in this rain they might get ruined. I'll deal with all that stuff later, when this afternoon is over. For now I have a nail file, I file my nails, I could make them round but I don't. Instead I file them into points, claws, like a cat. I could claw their eyes out; they would never be able to see me again. It passes the time, thinking about it.

I am a mutant, I can transform into a powerful cat, I am huge, I am scary rather than scared, they run from me but I catch them, shall I be merciful, shall I rip them to shreds? I laugh out loud, I cover my mouth, I mustn't make a sound in case they are nearby.

I wish I had nail varnish, black, with red for the tips. I distract myself again, I dig my claws into my own hand, it makes me stop thinking about the toilet, I keep digging, now the tips are red, blood red, it's beautiful, more so than anything I could buy in a shop; nothing could mimic that freshness. I lift my claws out of my flesh and look at them. I have a mirror, I line my eyes with my blood, it makes me look like I've been crying. I haven't been; what would be the point? I am already weak and pathetic. I might as well just lie here and die. I might as well anyway, it seems nice now, the thought, to drown in this little pond of flotsam, the rain is really coming down now, the water is all around me, I could just lie back and let it cover me.

I don't write on the walls, my claws can make a mark on me though, I write my initial, Y, I carve it into my arm. If I had ink I could tattoo myself. What mark do I want to wear for the rest of my life? I begin to draw another shape after my initial, a question mark, now it is Y?, it looks like Why? Why me?

Only an hour has passed, I must wait here as long again, when it is dark I can make a run for it. The cuts sting a little as the rain hits them; acid rain, I should be at home doing my homework, researching such things. They should too, I will do mine later, when I have managed to avoid them. I hope I'm sick tomorrow. Maybe I should take my jumper off, get a bit colder.

My mother, she'll ask me later, why did you take so long coming home? Why are you so wet? It's raining I'll tell her. I fell. Are you alright, she'll ask. I'm fine, I'll say. There's no point telling her anything else. She couldn't help. Are you telling me everything, she'll ask. Yes, I'll say, of course. I never used to lie to her.

I dig my claws in again, my other arm, I'm left handed and I'm using my right now, it doesn't look as good as the other one, but it's still my logo, Y?

It appears through my white shirt now; I'll have to wash it later. It's like a stamp, a label; at least this one I gave to myself. They wouldn't do anything so obvious, it isn't their style. I like to sit here and pretend I am strong, that I could hurt them. The fact the marks are on my own arms reminds me that I am weak. The pain is good, first when I claw it in, then when it stings in the rain. I wonder if it would get infected, were I to let it lie in the dirty water. I must stop thinking about water; how can I when it is raining and I am sitting in a puddle now, there is no point crouching, I am wet anyway, I might as well be comfortable.

My claws, like a cat's. A cat can retract them though, mine are here till I cut them, break them or bite them off. The blood is drying on the tips in spite of the rain; it is ugly now, brown, it doesn't look powerful and dangerous anymore, it just looks like something silly gone wrong. It makes me look powerful, feel powerful, when it is fresh. I dig in again, high up on my leg this time, I have to lift my skirt, I check first that no one is around, there are other people to fear than just them, no one looks down this little dead and alley, no one pays attention to what goes on in places like this. No one sees me, I lift my skirt, again I feel a little powerful making this symbol on a place no one else will see, not till I find someone I want to show it to anyway. This would be a nice one to get filled in with ink. Maybe I could do it myself, break open one of my pens, I'd like a nicer colour than the blue that comes in a biro though,

It's getting dark now, soon it will be, then I can go, I'll make a run for it, they won't see me so easily in the dark. I clench my muscles, making the marks is the only things that distracts me, that helps the time pass. I close my eyes, I don't even make a logo this time, I just dig into my upper arm, let the claws do their thing, I listen out for sounds, voices, people talking about their own lives, people who don't know I exist, a dog barks somewhere, followed by a yell, cars stuck in traffic, the occasional truck that makes the ground shake, my breath coming in, my breath going out, a little gasp as I must have hit a nerve, I feel clear, I can concentrate so easily like this, but only on the things I want, normally my head is so full of worries, I feel calm.

I should stretch, I'm stiff, I'll need to be able to run, my bag is heavy, it'll slow me down, I wish I could leave it behind, I wish I could leave it all behind, I should put my jumper back on. Cover the blood that leaked onto my shirt, people might notice it, they might think they are helping, they would just slow me down, make my escape impossible, strangers unknowingly conspiring with them.

I let the blood out into the water, it flows away, at first it is clear to see it, a little river within the lake, then it spreads out and all becomes one, my blood is everywhere and nowhere, blood is thin in water.

I pick myself up, lift my wet self up off the ground, pull my jumper over my head again, lift my heavy bag. The sky is indigo now, there are no stars, rain clouds cover it all. The light is orange; where it is, there are no streetlights here, that should give me a chance to get away.

I rinse my claws off in Cigarette Lake, I walk slowly out of the alley, feigning confidence, people walk by me now, they don't see me, they all have their own lives, their own problems to deal with, I'm shivering but walking helps me warm up quickly, I'll go to the bathroom straight away when I get home, the thought of home warms me up a little.

I hear a shout behind me, at least it's behind and not in front, they've seen me, of course they have they were waiting, I start to run but everyone seems to be going the other way, a solid sea of people blocking my way, I duck and dive, I hear footsteps behind me, I run faster, I turn down another street, down a hill, I move faster now, I still hear them behind me, nothing else matters, I can see my street, the last of the light is going now and there are no streetlights, they can't see me but it doesn't matter, they know where I'm going, they know where I live, it doesn't matter, I'm here, I'm on my street, I'm at my door, I fumble with the key, I get in and close the door behind me.

That's it for today. Tomorrow, I'll have to go somewhere else, hide somewhere else, do something else; perhaps one day I'll be someone else and then I'll be free.

The Produce Section
(Honorable Mention)

By Alan McClure

Picture the scene: an office of sorts, not one you'd boast about occupying; its false polystyrene ceiling punctuated by unsympathetic fluorescent lights, its windowless walls festooned with stock reports and staff rotas which are occasionally disturbed by a rotating electric fan. Corporate gray. Here and there this joyless décor is broken by a half-concealed postcard, one from Falaraki, another from 'California: the Sunshine State!' and yet a third featuring a picture of a cartoon ant with a beer bottle under the caption "All work and no play." Should this uninspiring prospect start to get you down, as it may very well do, your gaze might wander over the view, such as it is: this office, you see, overlooks the shop floor of Murchison's Hypermarket, a fairly successful food retailer in the center of Aberdeen. It can be oddly engrossing to watch people shop, you begin to empathise with the trance-like state the hypermarket's layout induces - not altogether accidentally either, as Toby Cartwright is high enough up the ladder to know. No, it's no accident, a lot of time and money has been spent on finding which colours, which tinny pop hits of yesteryear on the tannoy, even which smells, are most likely to raise the average shopper's susceptibility to advertising and so forth. The proles don't know of course, the shop floor assistants aren't told, but managers, even section managers like Toby, are let in on the secret.

This is Toby's office, and while he has no illusions about its congeniality he did work hard to get it and he keeps it in good order. There are bigger, brighter, pleasanter offices ahead of him, as long as he keeps out of trouble, and since doing otherwise wouldn't even occur to him, his prospects are good. Which is one of the reasons why this, this particular task he has to perform, irks him so deeply. Today, Toby's office is not quite as ordered and controlled as he likes it, because sitting across the immaculate desk from him is a manifestation of disorder in the making.

The boy is seventeen, he's been working at Murchison's for a year. Started out part time, Toby seems to recall, then went full time after leaving school at sixteen. A glance at the file: Danny Tate, produce assistant, good timekeeper, food hygiene certificate, customer care award (although to be honest you only had to turn up to get one of those), no previous trouble at all. So his presence in the office for a disciplinary warning has Toby (who's emphatically Mr. Cartwright for the time being) just a little unsettled. Add to that the fact that the boy is clearly emotional, and suddenly Mr. Cartwright's suit doesn't seem as comfy to him as he has every right to expect.

"So, Danny," the (section) manager begins, steepling his fingers on the desk between them, "why don't you tell me what this is about?" The boy shrugs. "Don't know," he mumbles with downcast eyes. "You don't know? Okay, maybe I should talk to someone who does know. I'll get Maureen on the phone." Cartwright notes with satisfaction that the boy's eyes have lifted in sudden dismay

"Aww, don't," he pleads. "Look, I said I was sorry, so can I just go now please?"

"It's not that easy, Danny," says Cartwright, trying to impart the fact that he wishes it were. "Maureen's put in a formal complaint about you. She says you called her." he glances at the note Danny has reluctantly handed him, and though slightly thrown by its contents he continues authoritatively, "she says you called her a crab, apparently." The snort of laughter from Danny is humourless and dry.

"I called her a cretin," he sneers.

"Well, a crab is a type of cretin, is it not? Why would you call her a cretin?" Danny just shakes his head, so Cartwright continues, "She also says you've been

damaging produce and wasting time. These are no laughing matters, Danny."
"I'm not laughing," comes the sullen reply.

Toby hates this type of thing. He's not a cruel man, he's not vindictive, and
Danny's record shows that he's a good enough worker: the Lord knows the staff
turnover in the produce department is fast enough, without actively forcing
anyone out. Turnover, in fact, has been even higher than usual since Maureen
Black became supervisor, though it's probably just a coincidence. Perhaps she
can be a little petty, but a good manager like Toby could never admit as much in
front of the staff. Still, he's inclined not to be too hard on young Danny if he
can help it: if only the young lad will toe the line.

"Look, Danny," Cartwright begins, then stops. "Listen, Danny," he tries
again, "are you happy working here?" The boy looks surprised by the question,
then slightly incredulous. "Are you?" he replies. This is just the type of bloody.
"Now look, that's just the type of bloody." The (section) manager calms
himself, but decides to abandon the friendly approach. "Don't make this worse
for yourself young man. Nobody likes a smart-arse, take it from me, okay?
Nobody likes a smart-arse. Now answer the question. Because if you're not
happy here, there are plenty lads your age on the dole would kill for a job like
this. Would you rather be on the dole?" Silence. "I said, would you rather be.."

"No."

"No, you wouldn't. It's no holiday being on the dole, believe me." That point
made, Cartwright decides to go back to the beginning, to try and unravel this
little piece of unpleasantness. "Now look, Danny, I'm not trying to threaten
you."

"Not bothered if you are," mutters the boy, but his knee is bouncing in
agitation and his breathing is heavy, belying the bravado and softening the
manager   sufficiently   to   allow   him   to   ignore   the   remark.
"Why don't you just tell me what happened, hmm?" Danny takes a deep sigh
and tries to control his breathing, hating the idea that anyone should think he's
bothered. "I made a man," he mumbles at last.

"I beg your pardon?"

"I made a man."

"How do you mean?"

"Out of a carrot, and some stuff." Danny's cheeks redden with the ridiculousness of it all, but he soldiers on. "There was this carrot, it was a doubler, and it looked a bit like a man kneeling down so I gave him a head out of a brussel sprout and a cape out of a cabbage leaf." Toby looks perplexed. Was that it?

"Well," he begins, trying to maintain his professional demeanor while inwardly cursing Maureen for her time-wasting complaint, "that doesn't sound like the best use of company time, does it? Making men out of vegetables? What were you supposed to be doing?"

Danny sighs. "There was nothing else to do. I done it all." Ah, now this is familiar ground to Cartwright and he smiles in anticipation of the oft-spoken speech he is about to make.

"Now that's not true, is it Danny? There's always something to do at Murchison's! Weren't there any sections needing filled, any customers needing help? I've been working here for fifteen years, and I've never once known there to be 'nothing to..'" Danny interrupts him, "Aye, but they don't like it, do they? Customers don't like it if you go and ask them if they want help, they think you're accusing them of shoplifting. There wasn't any sections to fill because I filled them all already, I'd cleaned the floor, I'd tidied the warehouse, there was nothing to do, honestly!" That 'honestly,' now, thinks Cartwright, was that a plea for lenience? Am I getting through to the lad? "Did you ask Maureen if she needed any help with anything?" He's trying to cover all the bases here, the composite professional.

"Yeah, she just told me to look busy. 'Look busy!'" he adds, in a squeaky voice evidently meant to represent Maureen's. Toby can't approve of that sort of insubordination.

"So what did you do?" he asks sternly.

"I went into the chill room. At least she can't see you in there. I was going to tidy it up but it was already tidy. But then I found the doubler."

"The.?"

"The doubler, the carrot, you know. The body." The boy at least has the decency to look slightly embarrassed as he says it. "We're not even supposed to put those ones out anyway, they just get thrown out. Maureen thinks they spoil the displays."

"Actually that's just company policy," corrects Cartwright, for some reason immediately wishing he hadn't. "Where did the sprout come from?" he asks, changing the subject. The boy looks sheepish.

"Um, well, I did open a punnet for it. I sealed it again though," he adds hastily. Mr. Cartwright is unappeased. "But you did take it though, didn't you? Do you think the customer who buys that punnet would be amused to think his sprouts had been." he searches for an appropriate phrase, "tampered with in this manner?" Danny is defensive.

"It was only one, Mr. Cartwright." The manager manages to control his anger; this matter needs to be resolved hastily, it is ridiculous and has already taken up too much of his time.

"That aside," he continues, "what did you do next?"

"Well, I gave him his cape and took him across to the wrapping machine and knelt him down next to the chopping board." A brief flicker of pride shows on Danny's face, then vanishes. "He knelt up all by himself," he says quietly.

"Everyone thought he was great!"

Cartwright breathes deeply, sensing a resolution. "And then Maureen came through the back?" he asks. Danny nods. "And what did she say?" The boy's eyes suddenly blaze, and his voice is raised in pitch and tone.

"She didn't say anything! She just picked him up and put him in the bin! And I went to pull him out again and she shouted at me to leave it and I shouted at her to fuck off, sorry Mr. Cartwright, but it, she, it was none of her business, he wasn't doing any harm and he was really good! He knelt up by himself! She's a bloody spiteful bloody."

"Danny! That's enough!" Toby Cartwright is not amused, a member of his staff has been insulted, and bloody spiteful bloody whatever as she may very well be, there can be no doubt that this is a serious issue. Still, the lad's upset. "Now listen to me, Danny. Don't you see that this is really just a silly wee thing? Maureen was right to discourage you from wasting the company's time. If Mr. Robertson or Mr. Hendry had seen your little carrot-man, who do you think would have got it in the neck? You? No, of course not. Maureen would have had to explain it." He lays his palms on the table and looks at the boy as this speech sinks in. The fan rotates towards him and rustles his forelock briefly.

"Now Danny. You're not really a bad lad, are you?" A shrug. "I don't think you are. But maybe there's just a wee bit too much imagination going on up there, where you should be thinking about work, eh?"

"Maybe, Mr. Cartwright," comes the subdued reply.

"Now, I see from your rota that you're opening up tomorrow morning, is that right?" The boy nods. "Well then, here's what you're to do. You open up the tidiest, fullest, cleanest blasted produce section that you can, so that when Maureen comes in at nine she sees what a good worker you really are, okay?"

Silence. "Okay?"

"Okay."

Mr. Cartwright stands up, relieved that the boy has chosen to be reasonable. No need to kick him out when he's really only just starting in the trade. "Good lad," he says, and offers a hand which the boy reluctantly takes, before turning and heading for the door. Just as Cartwright is sitting back down, Danny turns round.

"It's not my only choice, you know," he says.

"I'm sorry?"

"I don't think it's my only choice, this or the dole." The manager's mind is already drifting onto other things, but he has time for one last assertion of authority.

"Well, let's hope you don't have to put that to the test, eh, Danny." The boy leaves.

The next morning, Maureen Black notices something odd as she approaches the entrance to Murchison's, the automatic doors which open directly into her section. There is a crowd of people blocking her way, though it's only nine o'clock. Oh God, she thinks, what's happening - has some old dear had a heart attack or something? But as she pushes through the throng, she sees that it is worse, much worse.

All the stands have been pushed aside to make way for a spectacle which makes her blood run cold.

A giant mosaic of potatoes forms a rocky shore on the floor, with rock pools of grapes and seaweed of cabbage and lettuce. This breaks on an ocean of cauliflower waves, and behind it cliffs of onions and carrots climb the walls. Six hundred bananas are doubled in v's to form seagulls in a sky of tangerines, and apples are growing merrily from trees composed of date-and-fig trunks and vanilla-pod branches. Her entire precious floor space is obscured by this monstrosity, and every singly item of produce over which she holds sway has been used in the production of this outrage. Only one item is incongruous, peeking out of one grape rock pool: a plastic crab, on holiday from the fish counter.

Danny Tate is nowhere to be seen.

Neither Man Nor Beast

By Pamela Lynn Palmer

Pilar watched a pony draw a gaudy wagon through the streets of the small East Texas town. "The Great Armando" shouted the gilt letters. The sight of the driverless wagon drew a curious throng. Moments after the pony disappeared around the corner, a tall man in black clothes appeared, pushing a cart piled with boxes and trunks. Upon impulse Pilar followed him.

Armando suddenly turned to her, "Why do you follow the Great Armando? Does magic attract you? Beware of magic, she is a stern mistress. She will neither let me sleep nor love. You don't believe me, but you will see."

He whistled a tune and a small snake poked his head out of one of the boxes. Children began to shriek, but Pilar tapped the snake on the nose and he retreated.

Armando nodded approvingly, "Come with me and I will teach you everything I know."

Pilar raised her eyebrows, "We will see who teaches and who learns."

* * *

Pilar fidgeted in the wing of the theatre as Armando performed. Applause was meagre. At a pause in the show she ran onto the stage shouting, "The livery is on fire!"

The audience scattered to the exits. She assured him, "Don't worry. Your pony is safe. I couldn't bear to see you make a fool of yourself." She nodded towards the grumbling crowd filtering back into the theatre, "I will help you, that is, unless you wish to be pelted by rotten eggs and vegetables." Pilar looked very small in her plain green dress and bonnet, but strength of character shown in her eyes, older than her apparent years.

"Very well, you are welcome to try."

First she drew eggs from behind his ears. Armando yawned and the audience groaned. Then she tied a ribbon in her hair which burst into a glittering tiara, and the people clapped enthusiastically. She reached into Armando's vest pocket and out fluttered a small parrot which settled on his shoulder and croaked, "Arraugh, I'm Sam Houston, President of the Republic of Texas!" The crowd roared.

When Pilar passed her bonnet at the end of the show, it came back filled with Texas notes. Armando frowned, "These are practically worthless. We'll cross into Louisiana where there's real money to be made. That is, if you care to join to join me. You're a pretty good illusionist."

Pilar smiled mysteriously, "Those weren't tricks." She passed a hand over her bonnet and the money disappeared.

"Hey!" Armando stared at her. She pulled his wallet from his coat pocket. The notes were neatly tucked inside.

* * *

As the pony trotted along, Armando chattered to Pilar about joining a circus at the age of fifteen, performances in St. Louis and Philadelphia, and how he dreamed of touring Europe. Pilar nodded at the plodding pony, "Jester is tired and the sun's low. We had better stop and make camp." He pulled into a small clearing sheltered from the road, "Stay near the wagon and I'll gather firewood."

When Armando returned, he found Pilar stirring beans in a pot over a well-banked fire with a skillet of corn bread browning in the coals.

"So, you can make a fire. Did you set the one in the livery also?"

"It was a filthy place with sodden straw unchanged for weeks. Not fit for noble animals."

"A couple of broken-down nags and flea-bitten ponies."

"The horses were lame through no fault of their own. Anyone with compassion would have freed them. Now they'll build a new stable."

"And how long do you suppose that one will stay clean?"

Her glance silenced him.

After eating, they lingered under the stars while the pony, tethered a short distance away, cropped the long autumn grass.

As Pilar pointed out the constellations, her bare forearm gleamed in the starlight. Armando caught her hand, "The stars are magic. The leaves floating down, the rocks and trees, even the songs of the birds are enchanted by your presence."

Pilar pulled her hand away, "There is no magic without love."

"Pilar."

"No. What you feel is longing. Someday perhaps you will love."

As Pilar scoured the kettle with sand, the evening was shattered by the sounds of slapping leather and a shrill whinny. Pilar ran to see. "Stop! What are you doing?"

"Trying to beat some sense into this stupid nag's head. He crushed the toe of my new boot."

Pilar grabbed the whip. "You beat him, not for what he has done, but because I will not sleep with you and you dare not strike me. You don't deserve to be human and you haven't the nobility of a horse. Tonight you will sleep, and sleeping, dream. And when you awaken you will be neither man, nor beast until a child comes to set you free."

She grabbed Jester's halter, swung onto his back, and galloped away into the night.

"Hey, come back here! You know they hang horse thieves in Texas. Women," he muttered as he unrolled his blanket and stretched out under the stars.

* * *

When Armando woke the next morning, he thought his legs were tangled in the blanket. He noticed the scent of horse flesh, "Jester? Is that you, ole boy?"

He tried to turn on his back. He could turn above the waist but not below. He flung the blanket away and stared. Where his feet should be were horse's hooves. He lunged and struggled to rise. "I don't believe it. Damn! 'Neither man nor beast,' she said. God, please let it be a dream. That's it. She said I would dream. She must have slipped laudanum into the food." As the sun climbed higher in the sky, flies settled on his shoulders and flanks. At first he tried to slap them away, but then he learned to ripple his muscles and swish his tail. He practiced walking, trotting, cantering, and soon he was gleefully leaping fallen logs and ditches, swelling with pride in his new strength and speed. "All I need now is a lady centaur." Suddenly he felt alone. "Pilar? Hey, this isn't funny anymore. Pilar?" Shadows of fear crossed his mind, "I can't let anyone see me like this." He fastened the harness around his body and drew the wagon deeper into the woods.

By nightfall he was hungry with two distinct cravings: the man in him wanted meat and the horse craved grain. He settled on a repeat of last night's fare. He slept standing, with the upper half of his body nestled in the branches of a dogwood tree, padded with a blanket. He kept his rifle nearby even though the fire in the raised altar he built kept the animals away.

He woke to the rush of wind tossing the trees. Clouds flitted swiftly over the moon, and soon large drops fell. He huddled under the roof of the wagon, draped with oilskin as far as it would reach, while rain streamed down his flanks and sides. He stamped his feet restlessly. The shower halted at sunrise.

Wet leaves shone like diamonds. Mist lifted from the land. Through the trees Armando could see a deer galloping across the meadow. He grabbed his rifle and fired. The buck staggered and fell. Armando galloped forward, still carrying the gun, feeling the wet ground fly beneath his hooves with the same joy of strength the buck must have felt only a moment before. He slowed to a walk. He leaned down to touch the still warm shoulder. How like his own new coat was the velvety skin. Tears filled his eyes. He flung the rifle away, fell on his knees, and cradled the stag's head in his arms. The rest of the morning he spent cutting wood for a funeral pyre which he built around the stag and lit at noon. He ate nothing that day, and that night his altar fire became a place of reverence.

* * *

Years passed and Armando lived a strange and solitary life. He found a cave for shelter, read and re-read what few books he had, and spent most of his time tilling the soil and observing life in the forest around him. He raised corn and cotton from wild seed he found, built a hedgerow of dewberries, planted three pecans to shelter his burrow, watched them grow, and shared the nuts with squirrels. He made pets of raccoons and opossums. His hair and beard grew long and wild and he made simple clothes of the old blanket and hand-twined cotton yarn.

* * *

Armando at forty was old and lame, partly from a hard existence, but also because his horse body aged faster. One day as he dozed in the afternoon sun, he woke to find a little girl looking at him. "Please don't be frightened," he said.

"I'm not afraid."

"My appearance doesn't disturb you?"

"Papa told me there were strange creatures in the woods. He never told me there were any like you."

"I think I'm the only one."

"How sad. You're much nicer than a regular horse. My name is Pilar. Would you give me a ride around the meadow?"

"I'm afraid I can't go very fast." She climbed onto his back. "Do you like to be petted?" His shoulder quivered at the touch of her hand. As she clasped her thin arms around his waist and leaned her head against his shoulder, she felt him heave silently.

"Why are you crying?"

"All these years I have lived alone and never had friends except among the animals. Now I finally have someone to talk to, but you are too young. You won't be able to stay."

"I can always come back to visit you. Where's your house?"

"I don't exactly live in a house." He moved towards his cave.

"Do you like being a horse?" He laughed, "Actually, I'm a centaur. I thought they were only mythological until I became one."

"Then you weren't born like this?"

"A woman named Pilar bewitched me for beating my pony."

"My mother? She died when I was born."

"She looked very much like you. I don't think I would have learned as much as a man as I have learned this way. I was a magician, arrogant and vain. Now I know what real magic is. Every precious mystery of nature, is magical. Snow, lightning, birds hatching from eggs smaller than a thumbnail." He paused.

"A cave with a door!" Pilar slid off his back and bounded towards the entrance. She pointed at the wooden frame next to the door covered with a blanket,

"What's that?"

"That's my bed. I only sleep inside when the weather is cold or wet."

Going inside, she exclaimed, "Where did you get all this stuff?"

"I used to travel in a wagon. I made all my own magic props so I had plenty of tools. I made the door from siding of the wagon."

She picked up a book from a crate that served as a table. "Would you read me a story?"

* * *

Armando nodded drowsily by the fading fire. His legs seemed too weary to support his weight. He slid to his knees and lay on his side. His breathing became labored and the room swam before his eyes. He saw Pilar come towards him. The words she spoke floated away without meaning. She smoothed a blanket over his shoulders. Darkness drew a circle closer and closer around Armando until all he could see was Pilar's face by the light of a candle. Then there was only darkness and the rush of wind carrying him down an unknown stream.

The Villa
Third Prize

By Laura Owen

In the back seat of a blue rented car, a little girl sat, making up stories about her fingers. She often employed her time thus during long car trips. It seemed natural enough: each finger was distinctive and irresistibly suggested a certain personality. The middle finger was the biggest and clearly played some sort of dominant role; the ring finger was the most elegant; the index finger was less attractive but quicker; and the pinky finger obviously shy and retiring. She wasn't quite sure what to make of the thumb.

She had decided that each hand of fingers represented a family, but romantic relations could possibly exist between fingers of opposite hands. These relationships were often tragic and thwarted, not least because the poor finger-lovers were forever parted by physiology -- they could never hope to be on the same hand-though they could, sometimes, briefly, entwine.

She made up the stories about her fingers, in part, because she was bored. There was little else to do in the blue rented car. She couldn't read, because it made her feel sick; she couldn't talk to a sibling, because she had none; she couldn't listen to music because her parents were in control of the car's radio; she couldn't talk to her parents because they were occupied alternatively with consulting a large map and yelling at each other.

Abandoning her fingers to their destiny for a moment, she turned her attention the front of the car. Her mother was struggling with a large map, and fending off questions from the driver's seat, where the little girl's father was becoming more and more urgent and agitated. The mother's voice was beginning to quaver slightly.

The little girl observed the small clock embedded in the car's dashboard, and addressed her mind to another familiar car-ride occupation: estimating how long it would take, from any given point of departure, before her mother began to cry. That it would happen was an inevitability, but the timing varied, and the little girl suspected that this trip might make a record.

"But what do these crossroads mean?" her father was urging, "What does it say on the map? Which way do we go?"

"It doesn't have the cross-roads on the map!"

"Of course they're on the map! You're just not looking at the right place!"

"They're not! It's a large-scale map! You always just assume things a priori-"

The little girl had no idea what "a priori" meant, but she knew, from listening to pervious arguments, that her mother could not have chosen a more serious insult. She reached beside her and picked up a battered shiny silver notebook. Reading made her sick, but a little bit of writing was tolerable once in a while. Removing a pencil-also silver and shiny, and particularly treasured-from the spiral binding, she opened the notebook and wrote down, "Mommy's Favorite Words."

She never called her mother "Mommy" -- her mother discouraged it -- but it pleased her somehow to write down "Mommy," as if the audience for her writing was a different audience than her parents, some future stranger who would never know what she had actually called her mother. She tried to write "a priori" at the top of the list, but got stuck on the spelling. Each repeated attempt seemed more ugly and more wrong than the last.

"It's only supposed to be a few kilometers from the town! We've been driving for twenty minutes!"

"I'm the navigator! You have to trust the navigator! I can't concentrate on the map when you're shouting at me!"

View, the little girl wrote down. Shouting. Navigator. She got stuck on the spelling of navigator, too, and abandoned the list. The spelling was too much of a problem.

They had come to another crossroads. "Which way?" This from her father, angrily awaiting instructions.

"I don't know. It doesn't say-"

"Which way?"

The tears had started. "It's not on the map-" Twenty-three minutes. A record.

"Forget it. Forget it. We'll just go back to the town." Her father had stopped shouting: his voice had taken on the quiet, contemptuous quality that was far more dangerous than the shouting. He spun the car around, almost hitting a second car that was coming through the crossroads. He swore and raised his middle finger at the driver-her father understood the importance of fingers, too -- producing a horrified cry from her mother.

"Daniel! We're in Italy! They might want to fight you!"

Soon the same view was slipping past again as the car trundled back the way it had come.

Her parents collected Palladian villas; it seemed that practically every Italian town they stayed in had at least one or two -- in one case, a Palladian theater -- and they had now seen so many that even the little girl was able to identify distinctive Palladian features: symmetry, geometric shapes above the windows. It seemed to her that since they were all more or less the same, the loss of one should not be so upsetting to her parents.

"Wait a minute! Here it is! It's right here! The Villa Poiana, I'm sure of it!" Her mother tended to pronounce Italian with an exaggerated accent, something the little girl found embarrassing, though the Italians seemed, oddly, to like it.

Her father pulled the car over onto a red dirt driveway, revealing, in fact, a quintessentially Palladian villa, complete with symmetrical design, and geometric shapes above the windows. An arch curved harmoniously above the doorway.

"It was only a few kilometers away. We must've taken the wrong gate out of town." The mood had changed and suddenly her parents were co-conspirators again, exclaiming in amusement over their own stupidity. The car was soon parked and her parents immediately began rushing out of it, as if the villa was a train that would leave without them.

The little girl, though she had been bored sitting in the back of the blue car, suddenly felt reluctant to leave it. In her experience, buildings held her attention for less time than views. And looking at them involved standing up for long periods of time. The little girl did not enjoy standing up for long periods of time. After several hours in a museum, for example, she would begin to desire nothing more desperately than to sit down, and would stop paying attention to the art in favor of scanning each room for a bench that would not set off an alarm if one were to sit on it.

She got out of the car and trailed behind her parents as they chatted with the old couple who seemed to be in charge of the villa. Soon they were all inside, though the little girl has ceased to pay much attention to her surroundings. She was trying to decide what her favorite moment in Italy had been. She visualized herself writing in her silver notebook: Favorite Moment in Italy. Then the people, whoever the people in the future would be who would read her notebook, would know.

Suddenly, she realized she had lost her parents, in that they had wandered into another room and she was alone in the main front room of the villa -- no, not all alone, there was a security guard standing in the corner, near the door. She looked about her, trying to look as if she admired the furniture, or the pleasing proportions of the walls, which were covered in a sort of wooden paneling. She tried to look as if she was finding everything very interesting, from the battered trunk which sat in a corner to the large window through which she could see the blue rented car. Her feet had begun to hurt already. She had already ascertained that there was no where to sit down, probably one couldn't touch anything and there were almost certainly no pictures of food.

"Are you on vacation with your parents?" The security guard was speaking to her. She felt instantly embarrassed, as she always did when grown-ups felt obliged to talk to her. They needn't pretend that they wanted to. And why was he speaking English? Shouldn't he be Italian? She pretended to be deeply interested in the old-looking trunk -- it had leather straps, that ought to be interesting, somehow -- and mumbled, "Yes."

"And where have you been?"

"To lots of buildings." The girl looked up at the security guard -- or maybe he wasn't a security guard, maybe he was just a man in dark clothing who had been standing around with an air of studied nonchalance. He was heavy-set and dark-haired, younger than her parents.

"Buildings?"

"Yes. We drive to see buildings." The little girl didn't know why she was talking to him, but she was. "We get into the car, drive, for a long time usually, then get out of the car, see the building, and drive away. We drive to see buildings."

"Do you enjoy it?" The heaviness -- some might say the chubbiness -- of his face made him seem friendly. He seemed like a man who might work in the after-school program she attended.

"No." Until she'd said it, she'd hadn't completely realized that it was true. It was just something you did-look at buildings.

"You know why they keep taking you, don't you?" The man seemed amused, and the girl could not work out if he was laughing at her or not. Grown-ups were tricky that way.

"No."
"It's because they think that one day, you'll stop and think"-here he widened his

eyes and put an expression of dumb bewilderment on his face-" 'you know, I do like this building really!' "

The little girl started to laugh. She laughed because her parents were very funny and she had never noticed it until just now. As her laughter quieted, she reflected with satisfaction that she had always thought that she had a sense of humor and now she knew for sure.

"Come in here a moment." The man glanced quickly round him and pressed on a piece of paneling, which began to swing inwards, revealing itself to be in a fact a door, slightly smaller than the paneling frame. It was a concealed door, a secret passage. The girl sucked in her breath in delight. In her head she wrote Favorite Moment in Italy: Finding the secret door that led to –

But what did it lead to? The man waved her ahead and she scampered through, finding herself in a dimly lit room, apparently undecorated and made of gray stone.

All of sudden, she remembered that she wasn't supposed to do this. She wasn't supposed to go with strangers to rooms, secret or otherwise. A cartoon drawing ran through her head: a small child trembling; a menacing stranger in a gray trench coat. She'd be shown the drawing in school, during Safety Week. She was in that drawing now, she was the idiot child in the Safety Video that had accepted a ride with a stranger.

The paneled door slid shut behind them, scraping against stone. She wanted her Mommy -- no other word would do -- very badly.

"I'm just going to switch off the light." And incredibly, in the small stone room there was a light switch, and he flicked it off, and suddenly the room was not dim but dark.

"Look up," he said.

She did. Above her head she saw the ceiling was made of colored glass, and in the dark the sun came down and lit up a vast circle of blue and sparkling white. The glass made up a picture: it was a man, a man made of white glass so that he seemed to be made out of stars, shooting an arrow at a glittering stag who ran ahead, for now just out of the arrow's reach. It was not clear if, eventually, the arrow would hit the stag and claim it, or if the stag would ultimately escape, running away into the deep blue background. The man had a quiver, but it had no more arrows in it: his other arrows lay strewn about him, obviously products of previous, failed shots.

She examined the stained glass critically. Would the stag be able to escape this final arrow? The hunter was clearly no crack shot, since he'd previously been unable to hit the stag despite repeated attempts, even though the stag was really not very far away.

On the other hands, the stag had been shot at numerous times and had somehow managed not to move more than a few feet away. The stag needed to hurry up if it was serious about escaping.

But maybe it was enchanted, its feet bolted down by magic, or maybe it was person transformed into a stag, unaccustomed to their new body and unable to believe the danger. There were many possibilities that the spare space of the glass allowed for. It was very beautiful.

She wondered, though, if it depicted some legend she was unaware of, if there was a correct answer concealed from her by her own ignorance. Her mother would know. Her mother could always spell everything correctly.

"Does he hit the stag?" she asked suddenly, remembering what she had forgotten for a moment: that there was a grown-up in the room. The man did not reply.

The little girl kept looking up and wondered if it would be possible to float up to the ceiling and live there, to turn into glass and sparkle forever, running with the figures always through the cool, blue space.

The man moved forward.

The little girl kept looking up. If she kept staring hard enough, she reasoned, the arrow would begin to move, ever so slightly, the stag's feet would stir, there would be a rushing of wind –

They were back in the car, and her mother was looking at the map. "You know, I don't think that was the Villa Poiana," she was saying, "it's in exactly the wrong place on the map. According the map, there isn't even a villa where we were."

"Of course it's on the map, you're just not looking the right place -- just look over by the-"

"Who's the navigator?"

The girl was not listening. She was writing in her notebook, as she had been for quite some time.

After a short while, her mother folded up the map and glanced back at her daughter, who had remained more than usually silent. Observing her scribblings, she asked, "What are you writing back there?"

"A story," the little girl answered.

"Oh, good. Is it like Harry Potter?"

"No."

"Too bad. You could make lots of money and buy us a villa in Italy for when we're old."

The little girl did not reply. She wrote down "The huntsman's last arrow fell harmlessly to the ground as the stag kept running running out into the darkness."

Lessons

Second Prize

By Sheila Corbishley

"Someone's going to feel my hand today," Robert Duncan said. His tone was neutral, even pleasant, but his wife and children, sitting at the table, froze. Abbie, with a mouthful of Cocopops, found the whole lot had turned to cardboard, and Ben, skinny, clumsy Ben, began to cry, his face contorted with the effort of not making a sound.

"I think I'll have an egg, Susan," Robert said from behind the newspaper. "Boiled."

The test had begun.

Susan got up, knocking the table and grabbed the milk jug just in time.

"Oops!" her husband said jovially. "Watch it."

Standing at the fridge, with legs like jelly, she frantically ran through the possibilities: too soft, not soft enough, fragments of shell in the yolk - oh God, the permutations were endless. She could feel her breathing getting faster and shallower. Now she couldn't remember what to do. A row of copper pans glinted, dangling on their rack and she stared at them as if they had suddenly appeared from nowhere. Which one to choose? Her mind was a blank. Her shaking hands could hardly hold the little pan as she filled it at the sink. She let the water overflow in icy spurts over her wrists and watched the splashes settle in gleaming globules on the satiny steel of the draining board. Deep breathes; slow down. It was too soon. He liked things to simmer a little. She looked over her shoulder at the children. They were watching her with unconcealed terror, willing her to do it right. She managed to control her breathing and smiled at them both.

"Finished" she asked, putting the pan on the stove and wiping her hands on the cloth hanging beside the cooker. She wrapped her hands in its cheerful stripes to hide the trembling, and stood between the pair and their father as they slid down from the bench and sidled towards the door.

"Hey!"

Ben's face was ashen. He looked as if he was going to faint.

"Doesn't Mummy get a kiss, after making your breakfast? Poor old Mummy."

Weak with relief, they embraced their mother. Abbie's eyes were starry with tears as she gazed into Susan's face, searching desperately for reassurance; then with head bowed, she hurried out after Ben.

"And what about poor old Daddy?"

The mock self- pitying cry stopped them in their tracks. Robert watched over the top of his paper as they turned and came slowly back into the kitchen. They stood in front of him, waiting, while he folded the paper precisely, placed it on the table beside his plate and opened his arms. They entered as if ascending the scaffold, and dutifully put their arms round his neck. Susan watched fearfully as he held them tightly in a prolonged embrace. She knew that one fidget- the slightest withdrawal- could bring on the onslaught. But they knew, too: they'd learnt the hard way.

He held them until even he was bored and uncomfortable, then pushed them away.

"See you tonight," he said.

Susan returned to the cooker. The water was beginning to boil and her churning inside mirrored the seething bubbles. She rested her fingers on the pan handle, and for a fleeting moment imagined throwing the whole lot over him. In her head she heard his screams, saw him stumbling about, helpless with pain; skin peeling off like strips of cellotape.

Then she thought of his vengeance, and turned round fearfully. He was watching her thoughtfully. "Never mind the egg," he said. "Let's go upstairs."

The bedroom was full of sunshine and at the open window long voile curtains fluttered gently against a velvet button-backed chair.

"Victorian," he'd told her when they bought it; in a shop furnished like a stately home, full of gilt and tassels and huge ornate mirrors. "When did Queen Victoria come to the throne, Susan?"

He'd laughed with the salesman when cheeks flaming, she'd whispered that she couldn't remember.

"What can we do with them?" he'd asked indulgently, and the salesman, wary, had said he didn't know, sir.

He made it his business to educate her: Tests: "Keep you on your toes. Make up for leaving college too soon."

He was so good-looking, and got on so well with Mummy and Daddy. They'd loved it when he'd done the right, old- fashioned thing and asked for their daughter's hand in marriage. He'd flirted gently with her mother and deferred to her father. They'd been swept away - just like she was. She would never need to work, he'd told them. It was silly to waste all that time swotting for qualifications she'd never use. Better to be a good wife and mother - like her mother was. How proud Mummy had been, of her quiet, shy daughter. She had been proud too; she couldn't understand why her friends all hated him. She'd thought they must be jealous. And why wouldn't they? They'd had to stay on, plowing through their dissertations, while she'd left in a whirl of tulle and roses.

Geography, history, world affairs. Facts to learn. No opinions - she didn't need them. Fridays became a nightmare. She would watch other women in the delicatessen or the butcher's, her heart heavy with envy. She couldn't imagine being so carefree. They hadn't a worry in the world - stocking up for the weekend at the cottage, chatting about schools or the iniquities of nannies; complaining with laughing complacence about their husbands. She never joined in. Congress of Vienna, eighteen thirty-two. No! Eighteen . . . eighteen .

"Yes Madam?" the man behind the counter was cheerfully brisk.

"Eighteen fifteen," she'd blurted with relief, then pretended to join in the laughter that filled the shop.

There were other tests, but he didn't always tell her they were tests till afterwards, and then it was too late. She'd thank him in the long run, he said. It wasn't too much for a man to expect a little gratitude, was it?

"Thank you, Robert," she'd whisper though swollen lips, desperate to rub her mouth or touch the raw skin.

"You might smile when you say it," he'd say; "and go and wash your face and do something about your hair. You look disgusting."

The sun streamed across the bed where Susan lay. At the sound of the front door closing she struggled up onto her elbow and looked dully at her reflection in the dressing table mirror. He was right. She did look disgusting. And stupid. Stupid and disgusting. No wonder he got angry with her.

She lay back on the pillows and closed her eyes. A fat, furry bee flew into the room, buzzing aimlessly about before returning to the window; bumping fruitlessly against the glass, its drone getting louder.

Susan opened her eyes at the sound. She watched its futile bumblings until it rested, defeated, on the trembling gauze of the curtain. Stupid thing - it was so near the opening. Why didn't it just fly out?

She dragged herself off the bed and over to the window. The bee clung to the curtain, and she had a sudden image of Ben shivering on the side at the swimming baths, transfixed with fear; torn between terror of the water and the hideous consequences of disappointing his father.

She opened the window wider and shook the soft folds of net, but the bee hung on, its buzzing reaching chainsaw proportions.

"Go on you silly thing. Oh for heaven's sake, I'm not going to hurt you!" She brushed it away and it spun dizzily off into the drowsy warmth of the sunny garden.

Down below, Mrs. Lennox next door was hanging out her washing. Faint voices squawked from the little radio on the grass beside her. Women's hour. She gave a cheerful wave and Susan waved listlessly back; leaning on the warm sill, breathing in the scent of lavender and roses; sliding the tips of her fingers across the silky powdery surface of the windowsill. Then her fingers froze and her heart seemed to come to a full stop. Powdery?

She lifted her hand shakily and examined her talc-coated fingertips then dashed into the en-suite bathroom and vomited. Retching and gasping, she snatched up a face-cloth and stumbled back into the bedroom. She mopped the barely noticeable sprinkling of white powder from the sill then stared round, panting. Where else might have he put it?

With a wail of despair she fell on her knees and scrubbed frantically along the pristine white skirting board under the window; whimpering; peering into the toweling cloth for more incriminating traces.

She could hear him now: "Lucky old Mummy. I just wish that I could spend my days drinking coffee and flicking a duster. Don't you, Abbie and Ben? Hey - I've had an idea! Why don't we play a game? See if we can spot anywhere Mummy hasn't dusted. What? Oh dear! Oh naughty Mummy!"

"A house with children in it must be scrupulously clean, Susan. Would you agree?"

"Dusting is not a very arduous task, is it Susan?" Oh God, oh God.

She sat hunched on the carpet, shivering, kneading the damp flannel into a rag. When she felt the hand on her shoulder she screamed.

"Susan, Susan." Mrs. Lennox's round little face was wrinkled with concern.

"One minute you were at the window, and the next you'd disappeared. I thought you might have fainted so I climbed in through the kitchen window." She gave a little laugh. "I'd make quite a good burglar I think."

She helped Susan to her feet and sat her down on the bed, gently prying her fingers away from the scrunched up facecloth. "What is it dear?"

Susan turned her face away, flooded with sick shame. "It - it's nothing. I just felt a bit dizzy. It must be the heat."

Mrs. Lennox disappeared into the bathroom and rinsed the facecloth out. Susan sat limp and obedient as her neighbour wiped her face and smoothed her hair for her.

"This takes me back," Mrs. Lennox murmured, tucking the damp tendrils behind Susan's ears. "Getting my Chloe ready for school. She was such a fidget, though. Still is. She's a solicitor now, you know," she added inconsequentially.

"My little girl. I can hardly believe it."

She folded the facecloth carefully into a neat square, patting it into shape as she spoke. "You know, Susan, I've wanted to say this before, but somehow . . . well . It's just that I can't help noticing you don't seem to have many visitors. If you ever want to talk, dear . . just a chat you know -- just knock on my door and . . ."

Susan got up; her smile stiff, as if she'd glued it on. "Oh, no - no. Thank you, but I'm fine. I .my . we don't need other people."

"I see, dear." Mrs. Lennox followed her meekly downstairs and Susan unlocked the kitchen door. She felt an inexplicable pang of loss as Mrs.

Lennox's plump little figure disappeared, her feet slip-slapping in their flowered mules: back to her washing and her tall, cheerful husband. She heard the grating creak of the Lennox's back gate. Awful people, Robert sneered. Mrs. Lennox should expend her energy getting her lazy husband to repair their ramshackle gate, instead of trying to waste other people's time in banal chit-chat. If he knew that she had actually been in the house . . . Susan found herself glancing tensely round the leafy, ordered garden, as if he might suddenly pop up from behind a bush.

A yellow tennis ball lay half- hidden among the lavender and she picked it up with a quiver of relief. It wasn't like the children to leave anything lying about; Robert liked a tidy garden. Thank goodness she'd spotted it. She stroked the round fuzzy surface idly, watching the sprinkling of bees that hovered busily over the purple sprigs. Was the bedroom bee among them? She wondered. Robert wouldn't have let it escape, and he wouldn't have let her release it either. But she had, she thought, with a little thrill of triumph. And he'd never know.

She'd discovered the talcum powder too. The stirring inside her dissolved with a chilling rush when she realised that probably Robert had placed the ball in the bush. How many more tests were lurking? Would she ever pass them all?

She stood frozen in a daze of despair, the familiar whirl of panic engulfing her. Images hurtled through her mind - Ben's scream as he hit the water; his wild eyes as he bobbed to the surface; Abbie's frantic pleas; the droning, stupid bee that couldn't recognise freedom when it was offered; Robert, one eyebrow quizzically raised; his rueful smile . . . Robert.

She jumped as one of the bees detached itself from the lavender mob and buzzed past her nose. It flew over the hedge and she watched it longingly. If only she could fly. From nextdoor's garden she heard Mr. Lennox's drawling growl and an answering chuckle from his wife. They sounded so comfortable together, and safe.

Susan turned suddenly and looked at her own garden; the emerald lawn; the bright cushions of flowers. The fence was high and the glossy black wrought iron gate secure, but there wasn't an inch of safety in it. As if in a trance she went back into the kitchen. She cleared the table, filled the dishwasher, wiped the worktops; swept the floor. She hung a clean teatowel, ironed and crisp, on the little brass hook.

Upstairs, she plumped the duvets, smoothed the pillows and tidied and cleaned the bathrooms, then she walked slowly downstairs, fingers trailing on the polished banister. In every room the sun glittered on glass and silver. Through sparkling windows the shadows of leaves danced on carpets and furniture. The house was drenched in sunny stillness. In the kitchen she stood for a moment, feeling the tranquility wash over her. It was like standing in a stranger's home.

Then she took her handbag from the dresser, opened the back door and went out.

The Lennox's gate gave its usual protesting shriek as Susan pushed it open. She hauled it shut behind her and fastened the wobbly latch, then she began to walk towards the house.

The Leaflet
First Prize

By John Hulme

It was his turn. As he lifted Holly from her bed, screaming and thrashing, the hated cot death alarm went off, triggered by the sudden cessation of warmth and movement.

The alarm was more trouble than it was worth -- Steph's idea, thought Andrew.

Instead of worrying that Holly might die suddenly in the night, they now lay awake waiting for the shrill peeping of the alarm, or worrying that it had broken or that the power had failed, or that it wasn't sensitive enough and sometimes the thing just went off by itself anyway, waking Holly screaming from deep sleep and sending them both hurtling into her nursery in the madness of nightmare made real.

"You can't live by those odds. If you lived by those odds, you'd walk around all day expecting to get hit by a meteorite!" Andrew proclaimed. They were the odds of winning the lottery -- might as well be zero. There was no point in buying a ticket, Andrew said.

But sometimes he did buy a ticket.

He changed her in the pale pink glow of the nightlight. Moving automatically he was halfway through the sequence before he realised that she did not need to be changed, but he carried on anyway, a robot soldier too tired and primitive to adapt his program. He picked her up and carried her downstairs with cold feet, singing and shushing and bouncing as he went.

The fluorescent tube buzzed for a moment, glowed purple and then Andrew's unprepared eyes were stung as the kitchen filled with blinding light in a double flash as the tube finally caught. Something in his subconscious welcomed the light and the pain, as if they were expected - a long awaited release. He stumbled to the sink still bouncing Holly in that motion, which he was told, was comforting to her but which he thought might also have worked by coaxing her towards silence through seasickness.

He pulled the lever of the cold tap towards him and watched for a moment, half expecting the water not to come -- for there to be nothing but the rattle of a dry pipe buried in the walls and the rust flecked hiss of stale air. But the water did come, a clean stream splashing against the cold bright steel of the sink, swirling the little bits of baby rice that were stuck in the plughole. Holding Holly tightly with one arm, he continued the jogging motion and filled the kettle in a clumsy sequence of one handed moves: unplug the flex, open the lid, move the kettle under the tap, put it back down on the counter, turn the tap off, close the lid, plug in the flex, flick the switch. An enumerated list of tasks for something that, with both hands free, was fluid and unthinking. On the crumb-covered worktop was yesterday's post, which he had scanned quickly and put aside. Pre-approved credit card envelopes -- unopened but still there because he would need both hands to dispose of them. It was not a matter of simply putting them in the bin in these days of identity theft and credit card fraud. He would have to tear them to pieces over the bin, or take them upstairs to the study and shred them if he wanted to do a really thorough job. There were take-away menus and weight loss courses, the local free paper and - sitting on top of a postcard from Steph's mum in Majorca -- there was the leaflet.

It was white, mostly. Illustrated with colours that were not-quite-primary; more like washed out dayglo pastels. The font was free of serifs and curlicues as if some working group somewhere had decided that the utility of the leaflet would be impaired by the flourish of old fashioned characters. He had scanned through it quickly while waiting for his toast that morning. Interested, annoyed -- a little confused at first. Hadn't they just sent one a few months back? But this one was thicker and more detailed -- a practical guide.

He stood at the counter as the kettle began to bubble, varying his up and down motion with a sort of side to side swing, turning the pages one at a time. He stopped at a page that showed a line drawing in mauve of a determined looking man unscrewing a door from its hinges.

The kettle clicked off. He had not noticed the cloud of steam. He was too busy wondering where the screwdrivers were and whether the screws in the door hinges in their house were flat blade or Phillips. Holly sobbed quietly for a few seconds and then howled again as he stopped his rhythmic comforting and set about filling a glass bowl with water from the kettle.

He shushed her as he went to the fridge and fetched one of the bottles that was filled with the milk that Steph had pumped that afternoon. He lowered the bottle into the bowl to warm it and went back to the leaflet. Andrew turned the page. The man in mauve was now drawn in faded lime green as he took his newly liberated door and laid it at an angle against a wall with two other doors that had been similarly removed.

"What do you call a door that's gone mad, Holly?" Andrew asked hopefully. Holly howled in answer.

"Unhinged," said Andrew brightly and kept on juggling. It was worth a try.

Written at the top of the page in bold, clear type, without curlicue or serif, were words that sounded like they were from one of those leaflets that he sometimes picked up at B&Q, much to Steph's amusement. How To Fit A Loft Hatch. How To Rewire A Plug.

How To Plan a Fallout Room and Inner Refuge.

He bounced back over to the glass bowl, retrieved the bottle, shook it and then put it back in the water, before taking Holly on a short shushing and bouncing tour of the kitchen.

Fallout was a word from the world of his grandparents. Like lampblack or costermonger or tallow or chokedamp or Bakelite. An old word. Forgotten. His bouncing passage ended at the counter with the leaflet. He scanned the text on the next page, mentally ticking off items on the list as he went. Yes. Or at any rate there were some batteries in the top drawer in the kitchen, but he didn't know if they were the right size for the radio.

No.

No.

Two litres of Evian in the fridge.

He was pretty sure they had some of that in the garage.

No.

Yes.

No.

Could you get butter in tins?

He bounced over to the steaming glass bowl, took hold of the bottle, shook it again and squirted milk over the back of the tired wrist that was still holding tightly on to Holly. The temperature was just right. He put the bottle down, hoisted his weary and hungry daughter up with both hands, turned her around to sit in the crook of his left arm and then presented the milk-moistened teat of the bottle for her consideration. She took it straight away. Pulling on it with desperate strength, gurgling and snuffling.

"Hungry Holly?" he asked in weary satisfaction as his mind once again took notice of the sound of crying that was now suddenly absent. He joggled slowly back to the counter and turned the page.

For a moment it seemed to him that the determined man, now in radiant duck egg blue, was helping his prone companion into a very short sleeping bag that only came up to his knees, but in the next panel the determined man was pulling another bag over the head of the other.

"Secure the refuse sacks with duct tape."

Holly's clenched fist knocked on the side of the bottle in a futile attempt to somehow make the milk come faster. She had such tiny fingers but such a strong grip. Miracle fingers.

"The casualty will be easier to move if the wrists and ankles are first tied together with duct tape or shoelaces."

He felt something turning inside him. An angry thing appalled at these instructions, meant surely for a hit man or a serial killer, printed so clearly and with a bright a little sidebar labeled "Action Point: Ensure you are familiar with the correct procedures for dealing with casualties."

"Write the name and date of death on a piece of paper and fix it securely. After the fourteen day danger period you should take any casualties outside for collection by your local authority."

Andrew imagined the whistling and shouting of the bin men as they marshaled the wheelie bins, showering crisp packets and bits of newspaper around the close, picking up those strange, long, plastic-wrapped parcels left so neatly by the bins.

He looked down at Holly. She was entering a contented phase of her meal, drawing down the last third of the milk in long efficient gulps with only an occasional squeak or gurgle belying the imperfect seal between her lips and the bottle.

Behind his eyelids he saw his own hands take a pale plump arm that was wayward with its fist of miracle fingers and tuck it beneath black plastic. He heard the sound of tape tearing.

The postcard from Majorca slid onto the counter as he took the whole pile of post over to the bin and dropped it in, feeling somehow liberated as he thought of the pre-approved credit card envelopes that would soon be heading back out into the world unspoiled.

"The best defense is preparation," stared up at him from the back of the leaflet, without curlicues or serifs, in unpleasant brick red, now spattered with tealeaves and baby rice. The lid of the bin dropped shut. He heard Holly pulling on the empty air of the bottle and carefully took it from her. She did not resist. She was full now -- quiet and happy. He put the bottle down and carried her upstairs, facing over his shoulder, patting and rubbing her back as he did so.

In the nursery he unplugged the cot death alarm with his free hand and then pulled it roughly out from under the mattress by its flex. He lifted the lid of Holly's toy trunk and stuffed the jumble of wire and cloth and sensors down inside.

He laid her down in the cot and set the turtle mobile going. It played a gentle nursery rhyme with three notes. She lay there looking calmly up at the mobile and then up at him. People always said that she had beautiful eyes. They were wide and brown and there was no fear in them at all.

The Authors

John Hulme spent ten years writing programs for computers before deciding to target a more appreciative audience and write stories for people. He has just completed an MA in Creative Writing at the University of Newcastle upon Tyne and is now working on a collection of short stories and his first novel. He lives in Newcastle upon Tyne with his wife and baby daughter.

Sheila Corbishley has always told children's stories -- to her brothers and sister when they were children, to her own six, and to her primary school pupils, but writing them down didn't work. it seemed to flatten them. Then three years ago, the term before she retired, she joined a ten-week short story course at the University and discovered all the things she'd been doing wrong. Best of all, she discovered that she loved writing short stories. Even the exercises she's set in the Writing for Children class that she attends turn into stories for adults. Sheila hasn't given up on the children's writing though, and is a founding member of SSWAG, the Seven stories Writers and Artists Group based in Newcastle upon tyne.

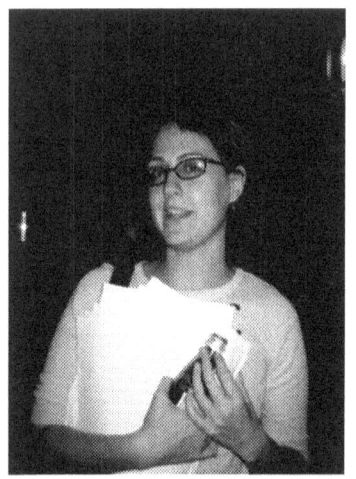

Laura Owen was born in Oxford, England, but grew up in America, mostly in Tucson, Arizona. She got her B.A. in English and Theater from Carleton College in Northfield, Minnesota, in 2004, and is currently completing her M.F.A. in Creative Writing at the University of Minnesota, where she teaches Literature, Composition, and Creative Writing. As well as fiction, she is also a playwright and has had several short pieces produced. She is beyond thrilled to be part of this collection.

Alan McClure is a 28 year old songwriter and ranger who lives in Dumfries and Galloway, southwest Scotland. He enjoys the short story format as a means to expand ideas which might not fit into songs, and has written several to date. Authors he admires include Alisdair Gray, Michel Faber, Gavin Maxwell and Kurt Vonnegut. More of Alan's writing can be found online at www.myspace.com, where he promotes the music of his band, The Geese."

Jason Jackson has been writing for four years. His stories have been published in a number of ezines, including pulp.net, laurahird.com and buzzwords.com, as well as in print by Cadenza and Slingink. For the last year, Jason has been a member of Alex Keegan's Bootcamp, an online writing collective. Jason lives with his wife in the South West of England, and he hopes to continue writing.

Leonard Kenyon is from Vermont where trees grow. Now he lives on a City block with a pretty girl and a pet television set. More can be read of Leonard online at www.writerscafe.org /profile.php?id=462.

Shannon Banks was born in Chicago, and lives in Surrey with her husband and eight-month-old daughter. As a Product Planner at Microsoft, she understands the challenges of balancing career and family. Shannon was selected as a runner-up in the Woman & Home short story competition in 2005.

Pamela Lynn Palmer is author of <u>Horse of the Dawn</u>, a young adult novel about the Nez Perce War of 1877. She has published three chapbooks of poetry, drama, fiction, and articles on history, folklore, and education. Her play Eclipse of the Sun, based on the Oxford as Shakespeare premise, was awarded "Best Play" in the Spring 2004 WriteMovies.com Contest.

Katherine Fay grew up on a farm in Buangor, Victoria with my Mum, Dad and two younger sisters Tess and Danielle. I'm a 21 year old Arts/Law student now living in a sharehouse in St. Kilda. A few of my favourite things: footy (AFL of course - go the Cats!), the live bands around Melbourne, reading, netball, writing and random road trips with friends.

Dropping out from the working world long before a socially acceptable age has left **Babette Gallard** poor, but also rich in terms of time and creational input. A habitual traveller, she is rarely at home and but always within in reach of a laptop to write her stories.

Joleen Kuyper was born in Ireland in 1981 and continues to live there in spite of the weather. She began writing stories as soon as she could read and is currently working on a novel. She lives with her husband, their cat and two dogs. Her other interests include cooking and eating good food, drinking wine, spending time with friends and family and gardening. Generally though, she is to be found tapping away on the keys of her laptop, wreaking havoc with her characters' lives.

Mark Fink has written and produced for television, working for every major network. He has written two Young Adult novels and several short stories. He lives Los Angeles, California with his wife Susan and sons Kevin and Eric.

Jordan Kushins was born and raised in southern California, attended university in Boston, Massachusetts and left her heart in London, where she graduated from Middlesex University with an MA in Writing. Her recent move to San Francisco introduced her to a brilliant but unexpected day job in magazine publishing. She writes because it makes her happy; this is her first writing award.

Jo Cannon is a G.P. in inner city Sheffield. She has been writing fiction for two years and has had some success in short story competitions, including firsts in Writers Inc, HISSAC and Libbon. Stories have been accepted for publication in "The Reader," "Tears in the Fence" and "Cadenza."

Jennifer Hill is a writer. She is pursuing her M.F.A. in Fiction at Johns Hopkins University and lives in Towson, Maryland.

A Canadian now based in Barcelona, Spain, **David Fulton** has had long experience as scriptwriter/director/producer on documentary films. He wrote the script for *To the Sea in Ships*, a two-hour film for Canadian Broadcasting Corporation followed by *The Beat of a Different Drummer*. Other scripts for CBC include: *The Icelovers*, *Animal Migration* and *Lessons in Genocide*. He also co-produced and wrote script on *Baikal: The World's Deepest Lake* (a Spanish-Finnish-Russian coproduction), and published articles in Canadian magazines: "Chatelaine," "Saturday Night" and "The Walrus."

Brad Adams has been writing since the age of seven, and has never lost his lust for the written word. Brad writes short fiction, novels, and the occasional play. Several of his plays have been produced around the United States, where he spent several years touring as a performer and director. Brad received his BA in English from the University of Texas, San Antonio, where he specialized in creative writing. He lives in New York with his wife, Aria, and their two cats.

Sally Hinchcliffe graduated from Birkbeck in 2004 with an MA in Creative Writing, having been part of the team who edited and launched the first issue of the Mechanics' Institute Review. She has had stories in the Asham Award anthology, Don't Know a Good Thing, and the first Tales of the Decongested anthology, and broadcast on Radio 4. She is currently living and working in London and putting the finishing touches on her first novel.

The Photographer

Reba Saldanha is a documentary photographer from Boston, MA specializing in people and animals in their natural environments. Her travels include India, Ecuador, Australia, Portugal, Spain, France, England, Germany, Ireland, Malaysia and most of the 48 continental states.

She has been a staff photographer for the Daily Item in Massachusettes for 4 years now and looks forward to more adventures through the lens.

See more of her photography on the internet at www.rebaphoto.com.

The Judges

Lucy Alexander is a writer and researcher on *The Times Magazine*. She read English Literature at Oxford, then worked in PR, becoming an account manager at Freud Communications before moving into journalism at *The Times* in 2001. She says of her involvement in the Momaya Short Story Competition: "Casting judgement on the work of other writers is an honour, a challenge and a big responsibility. I hope the Momaya Comp-etition continues both to raise the profile of the short story as a genre and to encourage writers from all over the globe to participate."

Claire Nozières works at Andrew Nurnberg Associates as a literary agent. Previously she was Foreign Rights Manager at Frances Lincoln, an independent publishing house specialized in high quality illustrated books and children's books. Claire sells translations rights to France for a wide-ranging list of contemporary US and UK fiction.

Rosalind Porter is an Assistant Editor at Random House and writes for the Spectator, the Times Literary Supplement, the Financial Times Magazine and Time Out. She is also co-editing a collection of new fiction to be published by Chatto & Windus in 2007.

Momaya Press

Monisha Saldanha Koruth earned her MBA at Harvard Business School in 2001 and has been working in publishing and internet commerce ever since. She believes that building a worldwide audience for the short story is vital to the promotion of this art form, and is proud that Momaya Press is increasingly recognised as the premiere forum for short story writers.

Maya Cointreau received a degree in Russian Literature from Smith College in 1996 and has more than 10 years of experience in publishing and graphic arts. Among other things, she managed *DCC Magazine*, a magazine with a circulation of more than 60,000 readers, and has published fiction and non-fiction works including: "Breaking Eight," "The Book of Cookbooks, Volume 2," "Equine Herbs & Healing: An Earth Lodge Herbals Guide to Horse Wellness," and "To The Temples: 14 Guided Meditations for Healing & Wisdom." She is currently working on her new book, "Canine Herbs & Healing."

Acknowledgements

We at Momaya Press would like to congratulate every author who submitted their stories this year – you are all fantastic, and you each had wonderful tales to tell. We encourage you to keep on writing, for through writing you become part of the divine cycle of creation.

A hearty thank you to our judges Lucy, Claire & Rosalind, and our pro-bono photographer Reba Saldanha, for joining forces with us and helping to create this year's review. Also, our thanks to Lynne Truss, the author of "Eats, Shoots & Leaves," for striving to empower punctuation in the English language and for sharing our sorrow for the apostrophe's mistreatment.

As always, a huge hug and a thank-you to our families, for whom our love spans oceans and miles, and kisses upon kisses to Maya's new June baby, Lucas, whose long naps and sweet nature allowed her to lay out this fine publication amidst smiles and coos.

www.ingramcontent.com/pod-product-compliance
Lightning Source LLC
Chambersburg PA
CBHW030338030726
47499CB00003B/818